LADY JUSTICE TAKES A C.R.A.P.

LADY JUSTICE TAKES A C.R.A.P.

CITY RETIREE ACTION PATROL

ROBERT THORNHILL

authorHOUSE®

AuthorHouse™
1663 Liberty Drive
Bloomington, IN 47403
www.authorhouse.com
Phone: 1-800-839-8640

This is a work of fiction. All the characters, organizations, and events portrayed in this novel are either products of the author's imagination or are used fictitiously with the exception of Gordon's Orchard. Bob and Kay Gordon have granted permission to use their names and their Orchard in this book.

First published by AuthorHouse   9/23/2009

ISBN: 978-1-4490-3200-5 (e)
ISBN: 978-1-4490-3199-2 (sc)
ISBN: 978-1-4490-3198-5 (hc)

Library of Congress Control Number: 2009909940

Printed in the United States of America
Bloomington, Indiana

This book is printed on acid-free paper.

Cover design and author's photograph by Margaret Thornhill

To my wife and best friend, Peg, who's always by my side and always laughs at my jokes, at least the ones she understands.

COMMENTS & PREVIEWS:

Britt Batchelor, D.C., F.A.S.A., Independence, MO. writes: "Loved the humor! Great escape from reality! Walt's character reminded me of my son's grandpa! Walt reinforces our belief that we should never stop dreaming."

Virginia Mulhearn, Raytown, MO. writes: "Laugh-till-you-cry hilarious! I really liked how the author developed the senior characters and made them heroes."

Rubi & Chip Schaub, Maui, Hawaii write: "Quirky. Laugh-out-loud, couldn't put it down."

Bob and Kay Gordon, Osceola, MO. write: "This is an entertaining book full of wit and humor. Bring on book #2!"

CHAPTER 1

I BELIEVE IN JUSTICE. At least I do now. There was a time in my life when justice seemed as mythical as a unicorn or a mermaid. It was something you really wanted to believe in, but seemed impossible to find.

I grew up in a small town in the Midwest. My childhood was typical of most kids my age. I rode my bike, played sandlot baseball, traded baseball cards and spent as much time as possible on my grandparent's farm.

You see, I was born in 1943 and when I was a kid television was new and exciting. My early exposure to justice came to me through my TV heroes. Roy Rogers, Gene Autry and the Lone Ranger dispensed justice in the old west. And who could forget the opening dialogue of my very favorite hero: "Look! Up in the sky. It's a bird! It's a plane! No, it's SUPERMAN, strange visitor from another planet who came to earth with powers and abilities far beyond those of mortal men. SUPERMAN, who can change the course of mighty rivers, bend steel in his bare hands, leap tall buildings in a single bound. And who, disguised as Clark Kent, a mild mannered reporter for a great metropolitan newspaper, fights the never-ending battle for TRUTH, JUSTICE, AND THE AMERICAN WAY." It still gives me goose bumps when I hear those words.

It wasn't until I entered high school that I discovered that justice could be quite elusive. Most grade school kids are about the same size and strength but as we reach puberty, nature has a way of segregating us into certain pigeonholes whether we like it or not.

Some guys bulk up and become football stars. Some guys sprout up and become basketball stars. Some of us get eyeglasses and become geeks.

And, of course, there's the girls.

Puberty has a way of changing one's viewpoint. When younger, we found ways to mix our spit with wadded up paper and fire the resulting spit wad at the girls with a rubber band. Puberty has encouraged us to expend an even greater effort to find a way to convince the same girl to 'swap spit' with us now.

That's progress.

While other guys were growing or bulking, I seemed to be stuck. As a high school freshman I weighed 120 pounds soaking wet.

I soon realized that the attentions of the fairer sex seemed to be drawn to the jocks and having had delusions of swapping some spit of my own, I decided to go out for the high school football team. You know what the old song says: "You got to be a football hero to get along with a beautiful girl."

I was issued a uniform complete with pads and helmet along with the rest of the team. As an incoming freshman, I had followed the exploits of our team for several years. Of course the upper classmen were the first team and all of us newbies were labeled 'scrubs'. The two stars of the team were Eddie Bowen and Gary Delong. Eddie was short and stocky, built like a tank, and could run like the wind. Gary was tall and lanky and could pull down a deep pass with the best of them. They were the co-captains of the team and everyone's hero.

Just as new recruits in the armed services or new pledges in a fraternity undergo hazing, it turned out that 'scrubs' were fair game. On the first day of practice, we were all dressing together in the locker room. First thing on, of course, was the jock strap. 'Gotta protect those family jewels.' Then the pads, jersey, helmet and shoes.

Fully dressed we proudly trotted out onto the field. I soon began to feel a 'warm' sensation coming from the area of my groin. The warm feeling seemed to increase at an alarming rate until I soon felt like my balls were on fire. I looked around and saw that my 'scrub mates' were experiencing the same. As if on queue, all of us sprinted toward the locker room leaving the upper classmen on the field doubled over with laughter.

After stripping out of our uniforms and standing under mercifully cold showers, we discovered that the first stringers had coated the inside of our jockstraps with analgesic balm.

Now where is the justice in that?

It was the next day that I learned a lesson in both discrimination and physics. Our coach was strictly old school. No coddling. Coach Gibler had the same philosophy as Harry Truman: "If you can't stand the heat, get out of the kitchen."

After calisthenics and wind sprints, which I handled quite well, the coach called us together and divided us into two squads, offense and defense. Our squad was the offense.

Offense gets the ball!

Cool!

We lined up on one end of the field and the other squad, which I noticed, was composed entirely of starters lined up on the other end. They were to kick off to us and we were supposed to catch the ball and sprint to the other goal.

Simple.

The high towering kick came right to me. I caught it and took off. It was just a few moments later that I learned a fundamental postulate in physics: 'for every action, there is an equal and opposite reaction.' I was pretty fast on my feet and I propelled my 120 pounds down the field only to collide head on with a 250-pound defensive tackle. I had as much chance as a Volkswagen crashing into an eighteen-wheeler.

Lesson learned.

And so ended my football career. Discretion being the better part of valor, one must know one's limitations and know when to quit.

All of the boys were required to take a physical education class. Unfortunately, Coach Gibler taught that too. Everyone had to 'dress out' except for the football squad. They got to sit out.

Not fair. We were all on the bleachers listening while the coach made some preliminary announcements. Eddie Bowen was there and in the middle of the coach's announcement he emitted a long and obviously forced burp: 'BRAAAAAPPPP!' The coach looked up, saw that it was Eddie, the football captain, and he along with the whole class had a good laugh.

"Well, hell," I thought, "I can do that." I gulped a lungful of air and blasted a burp that was every bit as forceful as Eddie's. The coach looked up, saw that it was me and I ran laps around the gym for the rest of the hour.

Where's the justice in that?

The balance of my high school years was productive in a geeky sort of way. Junior class president, President of the Beta Club, etc. etc. I soon discovered that girls were not drawn to academics but lavished their attention on the sports heroes. My dates, such as they were, were certainly not the hot girls in 'the club,' but were girls, who like me, were stuck with the bodies and looks God gave them.

How does that happen?

I had several really close friends, most of which were like me. Don was one of my best friends. He was a real 'brain.' While we both received straight A's, Don's understanding of things mathematical and abstract far surpassed mine. While I could fight my way through algebra, Don absorbed calculus like a sponge. We had a traveling chess set and we played between classes and at lunch. While I was at least socially accepted, Don lived in a world alone. He was really different than the rest of us in a way that is hard to explain. I lost track of my friend after graduation. I learned at a class reunion that he had taken his own life.

What a waste.

Eddie and Gary probably received football scholarships to college, married cheerleaders and are now hazing some other poor geek in the company they work for.

Where's the justice in all this?

By the time I reached adulthood, I was fairly convinced that justice as we commonly think of it is just an illusion. I came to realize that justice doesn't just happen by accident. It happens when good people make the effort to make things right.

The statue depicting justice is a woman wearing a blindfold holding a balance scale. So justice is blind. And the blind need a helping hand.

My name is Walter Williams and that's why I'm a cop.

"Hold on a minute," you say.

"You've done the math and have figured out that I'm 66 years old. Let me make it even more bizarre. I've only been a cop for one year! Please allow me to fill in some blanks."

In my early adult years, I did almost any job I could find. Then, on a whim, I took a real estate course and became a real estate agent. I spent 30 years selling houses and in the course of my career I acquired a number of apartment buildings.

Being a salesman and a landlord can certainly be financially rewarding, as it was for me. But it can also be very stressful, dealing with cranky clients and obnoxious tenants. So, after 30 years, when I was approached by a young couple eager to make their way in the world of real estate, I sold out lock, stock and barrel keeping only the three story brick apartment building in which I live and a rooming house which they wouldn't take. More on that later.

Ahhhh! Retirement at last. I didn't have to work. The income from the sale of my rentals fulfilled my meager needs and I own my buildings free and clear.

Now what?

One day, as I was leaving the Price Chopper Supermarket, I saw an elderly lady (look who's calling who old) across the parking lot heading toward her car. She had a bag of groceries in one arm and her purse over the other arm. I watched as a scruffy young man with long straggly hair approached her. Without hesitation he struck the woman, grabbed her purse and fled in the direction he had come, leaving the poor lady stunned and bleeding on the ground.

Where's the justice in that?

Then it dawned on me. I was finally in a position where I could give poor, blind, Lady Justice a helping hand and I decided then and there that I wanted to be a cop.

Easier said than done.

The building I retained as my home is a three-story brick walk-up on Armour Boulevard. It was built in the late 1920's and boasts all of the charm and elegance of that era. There are two apartments on each floor and a small efficiency unit in the basement. This being my home, I have very carefully chosen the tenants who now occupy the other five apartments.

Apartment 2-A is occupied by my college mentor. I met Professor Leopold Skinner when I attended the University of Missouri, Kansas City. He was the professor of philosophy and psychology. We became fast friends. Upon his retirement he moved, at my insistence, into my building.

Even today, at the ripe old age of 85, the Professor is as vital and lucid as many men half his age. One of the things that endeared him to me was his practice of not answering questions directly. Rather, he would quote some ancient philosopher, usually Confucius, and somehow the answer was embedded in the quote. But you had to find it.

When I shared with the professor my aspirations for being Lady Justice's newest recruit and the difficulties I might face to attain that goal, he simply looked me in the eye and said: "A journey of a thousand miles begins with the first step."

And so began my journey.

CHAPTER 2

I LIVE IN KANSAS CITY, Missouri, a large metropolitan area, and the police department is run strictly by the book. There are height and weight requirements and, unfortunately, age restrictions. Rules are made to be broken.

Right?

My ace in the hole was Captain Dwayne Short. We were friends in high school. Both Dwayne and I were of the same physical proportions, slender, but not skinny, wiry, but not muscular. I was 5'9" and Dwayne was a mere 5'6". Hence, the nickname that was bestowed on him by our ever-compassionate classmates, 'Shorty'. While I have stayed basically the same throughout my life, Dwayne experienced a growth spurt in his senior year and is currently a robust 6-foot tall. Nevertheless, the nickname stuck.

None of the men in his command dare call him Shorty, at least to his face. That honor is reserved for those of us who knew him when he really was 'Shorty.'

We remained friends over the years and I had occasion to do Shorty some favors from time to time. While he could be tough as nails, he also had a compassionate side. I have received many calls from him looking for a place for some poor soul to live while trying to straighten out their lives.

Now that's real justice.

I vividly recall the day I sauntered into his office took a seat and blurted out "Shorty, I want to be a cop!"

Shorty's my age and will soon retire, and here I am sitting across from him ready to begin a new career.

"You crazy old fool. You can't be a cop," he said. "You're too damn old."

"You're as old as you feel," I replied, "and I feel like its time to really make a difference with my life."

"Look," I said, "I know I'm not the typical recruit, but look me in the eye and tell me there is no place where a man of my age and experience can make a contribution."

He thought for a minute and said, "You really want to do this?"

"More than anything," I replied.

"I may have a way," he said. "The department is putting together a program inviting citizen involvement. Certain hand picked civilians are selected for the program. While there are no age restrictions, the program was designed for young men and women who are interested in law enforcement. They must go through the academy and learn police procedure. Then they may be paired with an officer in a squad car. Technically, you're not really a cop, but it's pretty close."

"I'll take it," I said.

The purpose of the CPP, that's the Civilian Police Patrol, is threefold: to involve the local community in law enforcement and invite cooperation and understanding, to find young adults who may become interested in a law enforcement career, and to add extra bodies in uniform to the streets without having to pay salaries from the tight city budget.

I don't think a 65 year old, grey haired senior citizen was their demographic when they designed the program. However, not anticipating that any old farts would apply, the restrictions were minimal. If you could walk upright and breathe and weren't a convicted felon, you could apply.

'Apply' is the critical word here. As I said, most anyone could apply, but to be an accredited member of the CPP one had to pass all of the entrance requirements of a normal police recruit. This involved a written exam, a physical and an oral review board. This, of course, was designed to weed out the insincere, the uncommitted, the faint of heart and old farts who didn't know how to act their age.

The written exam was a piece of cake. I sailed through that with flying colors. Of the twenty-seven original applicants, sixteen of us passed and were scheduled for our physicals the next day. Elated by my exam success, I returned to my apartment. I wanted to get plenty of rest, and as my Grandma used to say: "get up early, bright eyed and bushy tailed" and be ready for my physical.

I arrived at the Police Academy at 8:00 A.M. sharp along with the fifteen other recruits. I've had a few physicals in my day and I envisioned a kindly old doctor sitting down with me after a sweet young nurse has taken my temperature and blood pressure.

WRONG!

We were all herded into a locker room, assigned a locker and told to strip down to our shorts.

No problem.

It was then I noticed that the ambient temperature in the room was approaching that of a meat locker.

As we all stood around in our undies, the door opened and a uniformed officer entered. "All right men," he barked, "form a single line, drop 'em and stand at attention."

Say What!!

I have to admit that I hadn't been totally naked in a roomful of men since my locker room days in high school, but what the hell. So I dropped them.

There's a funny thing about guys and their manhood. There seems to be an inborn curiosity about how they stack up compared to the next guy. But it's not polite to look. You will see ten guys lined up side by side at the urinals at the ballpark and if you watch closely they will always try to sneak a peek.

So there we were, sixteen guys, standing at attention buck-naked trying not to look at the fellow standing next to us.

Now remember, I'm 65 years old. Body parts tend to shrink as you age. It's a medical fact. I weigh all of 145 pounds and I'm standing in a friggin' meat locker. I couldn't help but sneak a peek at the 22-year-old stud standing next to me. I looked down and 'YIKES' when did I become a eunuch? As if that wasn't bad enough, I also noted that I was the only one in line whose pubic hair was grey.

Just when I thought it couldn't get any worse, the door flew open and in stepped Nurse Ratchet. It had to be her. Straight out of One Flew Over The Cuckoo's Nest. "Oh Shit," I thought, I couldn't believe I could shrink up any more, but somehow, I did. It didn't make me feel any better when I saw her snap on a pair of rubber gloves.

This can't be good.

She stepped up to the first guy in line, looked in his eyes, ears and mouth then squatted down and in one smooth motion grabbed the guy's balls and shoved them up into his groin. "Turn your head and cough," she ordered. A gasp of horror was heard all down the line. "Now, turn around, bend over and spread 'em," she ordered.

Spread What?

I was the next to last guy in the line so I got to wait and watch the humiliation as she proceeded down the line. After examining fourteen young, fit, nubile specimens of manhood, she came to me. Eyes, ears, throat. Then she bent down and I held my breath as I awaited my fate. I looked down and she was grinning from ear to ear. She looked up, gave me a wink and plunged. I guess I had made her day.

There's nothing like being naked in front of strangers and having your body parts probed by a Neanderthal in rubber gloves to give one a sense of humility. As I left the Academy, I was feeling pretty humble. But I had passed. Two down and one to go.

All that was left was the oral exam by the review board. I had received a call from Shorty asking me to come by his office. He frankly told me that the review board had concerns about my admittance. They thought I would have washed out by now, but having passed the written and physical exams, all that stood between me and the CPP was the review board. "Walt," he said, "you know you have my support and several of the other Captains are on the fence, but Captain Harrington wants you out. He's going to give you a rough time at the review. If you can't provide answers to his questions, you'll be out."

Shorty explained that it was the boards' job to make sure that any new recruit could handle himself in dangerous or life threatening situations and he gave me a few hints as to what questions would be asked.

Most cops you see on the street are young, strong and physically capable of handling the confrontations they face on a daily basis. I'm none of those things. But if you're going to succeed, you use the tools that God has given you. If you can't beat them up, you'd better be able to outsmart them.

At home that evening, I shared my trepidations with the Professor. He thought for a moment about my upcoming confrontation with Captain Harrington and simply said: "Wise man never play leapfrog with unicorn."

What I needed was an equalizer.

I arrived at the Academy and was escorted to the conference room. Seated around the table were the Captains of the various squads, narcotics, vice, canine, foot patrol, etc. Shorty introduced me and each Captain in turn asked me questions about my background and my motivation for being part of the CPP.

So far, so good.

Finally it was Captain Harrington's turn. "Mr. Williams," he began, "it is my opinion that you have no business taking part in this program. First, you're too damn old. My father is your age, for chrissakes. If you are so determined to give public service you should volunteer at the senior center. All you are going to do is get in the way and get yourself hurt."

I noticed the other Captains had lowered their heads and were embarrassed by his belligerent attitude.

"Think about it old man," he continued. "Let's say you are making a routine traffic stop. You ask the driver for his license and registration and he says, 'Fuck you.' You ask him to step out of the vehicle and he does, all 250 pounds of him and he's got a blade in his hand. Whadda you gonna do?" he bellowed. "Whadda you gonna do old man? Whadda you gonna do?" And he jumped up from his seat and started toward me.

"Well, it's all or nothing," I thought. And without a word, I reached into my pocket, pulled out a Benford #5 taser, aimed and pulled the trigger.

Two small probes attached to the taser by high voltage insulated wire struck the Captain squarely in the chest and delivered a 50,000-volt electric shock. His body tensed, his eyes rolled back in his head and he hit the ground like a sack of dog food. The other captains looked on in horror as Harrington lay writhing on the floor. In a moment their shock subsided and I thought I detected a smile forming on their lips. Suddenly their smiles turned to outright laughter and a round of applause circled the table.

At that moment, one of the Professor's witticisms popped into my mind: "Man who behaves like an ass will be the butt of those who crack jokes."

Shorty stood, took my hand in his and said. "Congratulations Walt, and welcome to the CPP."

CHAPTER 3

I HAD BEEN DREADING the next step in my induction process. PT, that's physical training, an acronym for getting your ass kicked.

By this time, ten of the original twenty-seven had made the cut and we gathered in the gymnasium. Two guys came into the room dressed like Ninjas and lined us up around a mat on the floor. They explained that their job was to teach us some basic hand-to-hand combat skills so that we could protect ourselves and subdue the bad guys. Unfortunately my reputation preceded me and they made me leave my taser in the locker room. I was on my own.

The two Ninja guys squared off and began a series of intricate ducks and parries and jabs. Now it was our turn. I watched as the first recruit was attacked by the instructor. He was soon flat on his back gasping for air.

"Don't hold back," the Ninja said. "This may well be a life or death situation. Don't worry about hurting us. Protect yourselves."

One by one each recruit took their turn getting their ass handed to them on a platter.

Finally, I was up. "If these young studs are getting the crap kicked out of them, what chance do I have?" I wondered. Then a thought came into my mind and a little voice said, "If you can't whup 'em you'd better outsmart 'em." Kinda like Yoda in Star Wars. "May the force be with me," I thought as I took the mat.

I was dancing around the mat doing my best to avoid physical contact. You know 'float like a butterfly, sting like a bee' when I remembered a scene from a movie I had seen. What I needed was a distraction. Then I could move in for the kill. I pointed down to his feet and said, "Be careful, I think your shoe's untied."

Instead of looking down as I was, he delivered a roundhouse to the side of my head. Some guys just can't follow a script. I remember in the comics I read as a kid, when some character was whacked he always saw stars. I thought that was really funny.

Not so much.

As I lay on the floor, it suddenly occurred to me in which movie I had seen that particular diversion, <u>The Three Stooges.</u>

Ok, what now? Here I am in a fetal position waiting for the Ninja to come in for the kill. Think! Think! Then it came to me, 'if you can't be a grizzly, be a possum' and remembered a quote from my mentor: "Man who gets kicked in testicles left holding bag."

The Ninja guy stood over me and yelled, "Get up old man," and he gave me a kick in the ribs. I lay motionless on the floor not moving a muscle. Again, "I told you to get up."

Nothing.

Fearing he had crippled a senior citizen the Ninja spread his legs apart, straddled my body and bent down to see if I was still breathing. I kicked upward with all my strength and planted his gonads halfway up his ass. He moaned, grabbed his crotch and fell to the mat. I was immediately on top of him, my forearm pressed against his throat bearing down with all my 145 pounds.

Out of all the recruits that day, only the old dude whupped the Ninja. "Well done Obe Wan Knobe."

The last obstacle was to be certified with a firearm. We were taught basic handgun techniques and had to qualify at the range to get our permit to carry. I wasn't too concerned about qualifying. I had been hunting since I was a kid on my grandpa's farm. The 45mm Glock was the standard police issue. We went to the firing range, put on our ear protection and the range officer handed me the Glock.

"Damn, this thing must weigh 10 pounds," I said. I chambered a round, held the gun with both hands, aimed at the target and pulled the trigger. 'BLAM!' The recoil forced my arms up about a foot, my hand jerked on the trigger firing off another round which took out a light in the ceiling above the target. "Whoa! This thing could stop an elephant."

I could see that qualifying with this bazooka was going to be a problem, so, back to my old pal Shorty. After studying the regulations for the CPP, he concluded that the requirement was only to qualify on the range. No specific handgun was mentioned. It just so happened that I had my own revolver.

I was a young dude and had just moved to Kansas City from my hometown. I was awed by its size and honestly a little bit scared, so I went to the local pawn shop and bought a .25 caliber semi-automatic, just in case. At that time I lived in a small efficiency apartment above Schuler's Drug store at 45th and State Line. Fortunately, by the time I returned home the drug store was closed. I unpacked my .25, loaded the clip, slammed it in and pulled back the slide. When I let go, 'BLAM!' I shot a hole in my coffee table and the slug penetrated my floor, which coincidently was also the ceiling of the drug store. I heard a crash below. That's not supposed to happen.

I wrapped up the .25 and hotfooted back to the pawnshop. "This isn't going to work," I told the clerk. "I damn near blew off my foot. Don't you have anything else?"

"I've got just the thing," he replied. He went to the backroom and came out with a revolver that looked just like the one Roy Rogers carried.

Perfect.

"Wow, six shooter," I said.

"Not really," he replied. "This shoots .22 caliber long rifle shells and because they are a smaller shell there is room in the cylinder for 9 bullets."

Cool!

I dropped by Schuler's Drug store the next morning. Mr. Schuler was mopping the aisle. "What happened?" I asked.

"Damndest thing," he said. "When I opened up this morning Pepto Bismol was all over everything. Looks like the damn display just exploded."

"Wow, that is weird," I replied. He never figured it out and I never told.

I love that gun. I've hunted rabbits and squirrels and other varmints with it over the years and have become a pretty decent shot. Now I was ready for varmints of the two-legged variety.

I showed up at the range the next day, qualified, and was ready to begin my new career in law enforcement. Lady Justice, you can rest easy now. Walter Williams is on duty. "Hi Ho Silver, Awaaaaay!"

CHAPTER 4

THE NEXT DAY I REPORTED to the squad room at police headquarters at 12th and Oak in downtown Kansas City.

Captain Short introduced me to the squad and explained my presence there in the CPP program. I was greeted with a smattering of applause, a few finger waves, and, unfortunately, a few frowns. Apparently not everyone was as excited about my new career as I was. Some glared at me. Most didn't give a damn.

After roll call and daily assignments the room emptied except for me and one other uniformed officer.

"Walt," Captain Short said, "I'd like you to meet your new partner, George Wilson."

This huge guy stood up and started my way. He was a full 6'2" and had to weigh at least 220. He was barrel chested and his uniform buttons strained to hold in his bulging muscles. He kind of reminded me of Dr. David Banner just as he's turning into the Incredible Hulk.

He held out his huge hand, which completely engulfed mine and said, "Just call me OX. Everybody else does." And so began a partnership and friendship that has endured the test of time.

Ox is a 22-year veteran, all as a patrol officer. He has never sought nor has he been offered a higher rank. He is not the sharpest tack in the corkboard, but with 22 years on the streets of Kansas City, he knows his job. As a private citizen, Ox is the kind of cop I would want standing between me and the scum that roam the streets. His primary duties include regular patrol duty in the downtown K.C. area, crowd control at crime scenes, and the service of bench warrants from the Court.

We walked to the motor pool and Ox opened the door to a black and white Crown Vic that looked like it had been in service as long as he had. "Welcome to car 54," he said, and we were on our way.

We cruised the streets of downtown Kansas City, hoping to deter crime by our mere presence. Ox waived at the newsstand boy, the boy with the hot dog wagon and the meter maid. He was a regular fixture on Grand Avenue.

Suddenly the two-way radio erupted, "Domestic violence reported in the eighteen hundred block of Campbell. Woman screaming. Any units nearby please respond."

Ox keyed the mike, "Unit 54 at 14th and Grand responding. ETA 6 minutes."

"Roger that 54, over and out."

With that, Ox flipped on the lights and siren and in 5 minutes we were on Campbell. It wasn't difficult to find the disturbance. As we cruised the block, a woman's shrill scream erupted from the second floor of 1814 Campbell. We parked and ran through the entrance and up the steps to the second floor.

Ox knocked on the door, "Police! Open the door, please," he shouted. No response. This time a louder knock. "This is the police. Please don't make me bust down your door 'cause I AM coming in."

We heard a muffled voice and a whimper and a bolt slide on the door. A large fat man opened the door. He was wearing a dirty T-shirt that strained against his beer belly. His hair was greasy. He hadn't shaved for days. He was holding a carton of Chinese take-out. He looked at us through yellow eyes. "Whadda you want?" he said.

"Sir, we had a domestic disturbance call at this location. We need to come in and check things out," Ox replied.

"The hell you will," he said.

Ox peered over his shoulder and saw a slender woman in a worn housedress cowering in the corner. Her eye was black. Her nose was bleeding and she was holding her ribs. "Ma'am, are you all right?" Ox asked. "What's going on here?" No answer.

"This ain't no big deal," the man said. "I was just teaching the little lady here a lesson. I told her to order cashew chicken and the dumb bitch got chicken rangoon. She's gotta learn."

"Sir, step aside. I'm coming in," Ox ordered.

And in response, the man launched the box of Chinese right at Ox's head. Ox ducked. He's incredibly fast for a big man. The box exploded on MY chest and I was covered from head to toe with chicken rangoon.

I don't even like Chinese.

No more Mr. Nice Guy. Ox launched himself at the fat man hitting him square in his beer belly. He let out a 'WHOOOOF' and down he went. Ox rolled him onto his stomach and was in the process of cuffing him, when, out of the corner of my eye, I saw the woman coming at Ox's back with a lava lamp poised over her head.

Having seen Ox in action I figured I'd better do the same. My intent was to tackle the woman before she bashed in the back of Ox's head.

Unfortunately, I did not take into account the slippery rangoon on the floor. My feet went out from under me, but my momentum carried me right into Ox.

As we both went down in a heap, the woman was on the downswing. With Ox no longer there, the lava lamp smashed against the fat man's greasy head and exploded. Runny blue glop covered his head and shoulders. I always wondered what was in one of those things.

See, there really is justice if you help the blind lady along.

The woman was screaming, "What have you done?"

"I think we just saved your ass," I said.

"The hell you have," she said. "Now get outta here and leave us alone."

"But don't you want to press charges?" I asked.

"No, now get outta here!" she screamed.

I looked at Ox and he just shook his head. "I'll never understand," he said. "These poor women get the crap beat out of 'em on a regular basis. But they just keep coming back for more. They can't seem to break away without a lot of intervention."

Fortunately, the law says that in the case of domestic violence, if the victim will not file a complaint, the officer on the scene may do so at his discretion. Besides, he's gonna be up for assaulting a police officer with a deadly weapon.

That rangoon was NASTY!

So we cuffed the fat guy, hauled him down to the station, and got him booked. Ox gave the name of the woman to Social Services. We can only hope she gets the help she needs.

I was in the locker room changing into clean clothes when a uniform stuck his head around the corner and yelled. "Hey! Williams! How about bringing me an order of chow mien. Maybe you could throw in an egg roll." And off he went laughing his ass off. Word gets around fast in the precinct.

By the time we finished the paperwork it was lunchtime. We munched a vending machine sandwich from the break room and were off again to 'serve and protect' the good citizens of Kansas City.

CHAPTER 5

ABOUT MID AFTERNOON A CALL came through to all units in the downtown area. There had been an armed robbery at the Stockyards building in the West Bottoms. Kansas City is the hub of livestock distribution and sales in the Midwest. Farmers from several surrounding states bring their cattle, hogs, sheep and other four-legged creatures in to market. Large packinghouses like Swift and Armour purchase many of the animals for slaughter and meat processing. The animals are kept in corrals surrounding the multistoried Livestock Exchange Building.

When we arrived on the scene, Detectives were busy securing the area around the building. The Detective in charge from robbery was Bill Grainger. "Good to see you guys," he said as we drove up. "We could use you two to help cordon off the area and keep the gawkers back."

"What happened?" Ox asked.

"Two men wearing gray jumpsuits and red nylon stockings on their heads robbed the Exchange office," Grainger said. "There was a big sale today and they made off with a wad of cash. They can't be too far away. A clerk triggered a silent alarm and we responded in minutes. We've got every available man searching the area."

We helped erect the crime scene tape and stood guard as a large crowd began to gather. There was no pushing or shoving. Just curious people with boring lives hoping for a vicarious thrill.

As I was surveying the crowd, a grey jumpsuit caught my eye. I looked closer and saw what I initially thought was a red bandana sticking out of a back pocket. I looked again. "My God! That's not a bandana. It's pantyhose." Either that guy had just come from a shopping spree at Victoria's Secret or he was our perp. Pretty clever. They knew they were surrounded, so the best place to hide is in plain sight. Right? Just blend in with the crowd while the cops are busting their asses searching the area.

I leaned over to Ox. "Look," I said, and pointed to Mr. Pantyhose.

At that moment our eyes met and he realized he had been made. He grabbed his cohort and off they sprinted toward the livestock pens.

Ox and I took off in hot pursuit. As they reached the pens they split up, going in opposite directions. Ox went left and I went right. I saw my guy with the red pantyhose hanging out his ass, scale a fence and disappear.

Without giving much thought I scaled the fence as he had and as I was straddling the top board I found myself looking down at the perp standing in the middle of the corral. A 9mm Beretta was pointed right at my head.

They didn't cover this at the Academy.

I was thinking my career in law enforcement was about to come to a premature end when I noticed movement in the far corner of the corral. A huge Black Angus bull had emerged and was pawing the ground. His attention seemed to be focused on the perp's ass.

THE RED FLAG!

BULL!

All right! But please do it NOW!

The perp's attention had been entirely on me and too late he turned as he heard the thundering hoofs of Mr. Quarterpounder.

'WHAM!' The bull hit him square in the butt. The Beretta flew one direction as he was launched about six feet in the air. 'WHOOF!' He hit the ground and while the bull's attention was still on its conquest, I scurried down and retrieved the gun. I fired a round into the ground and the bull, startled, retreated to the far end of the corral. I grabbed my cuffs, fastening one end to the perp's hand and the other to the metal gatepost. I pulled the red stocking from his back pocket and hung it on the fence next to him but just beyond his reach. I figured Mr. Bull might as well stand guard until I could get back.

I scaled the fence and ran in the direction I last saw Ox. I heard voices coming from a stall and I cautiously peeked through the slats in the fence. Apparently the perp had gotten the drop on Ox just as his buddy had with me. Ox was on his knees and the perp had a gun pointed at his head. I looked around. No red flag. No bull. "CRAP!"

YES CRAP!

The stall they were in was apparently in the process of being mucked when the robbery occurred. The guy running the loader had been ordered to stop so the cops could secure the area. He had left the loader suspended in mid-air filled to the brim with steamy cow poop. Like my perp not noticing the bull, this guy was so focused on Ox he didn't realize he was standing directly under the bucket.

I had never operated a high loader before. It can't be too hard. Guys with big necks do it. So I cautiously slipped into the driver's seat. "Geesh. How many levers does this thing have?" I pulled the first lever. Nothing. I pulled the second lever. Nothing. I pulled the third lever and BINGO – JACKPOT.

The perp heard the big bucket groan and as it swung down to release its steamy load, the perp looked up and opened his mouth to scream.

Wrong thing to do.

"OH SHIT!" he screamed, as the waste of a hundred heifers cascaded on his upturned face.

"Yep, you're right," I thought. You see, Lady Justice also has a sense of humor.

Ox got up from his knees, took my small hand in his large paw and held on for a long time.

Not too bad for my first day on the job.

CHAPTER 6

I WAS FEELING PRETTY GOOD as I drove back to my apartment building. As I turned into the drive, I saw my old friend Willie Duncan sitting on the front stoop.

Willie has been with me nearly 20 years now. I first met Willie while shopping for electrical supplies for one of my rentals. I was told Willie had a good supply of fixtures and I could find him at 12th and Garfield.

I assumed that he had a storefront there, but as I drove up I saw a wiry little black guy sitting on the bumper of his car with the trunk popped open. It turned out that Willie was a petty thief and a con artist. He was very good at his trade. He was one of those guys that operated just under the radar. He picked his targets carefully and left no clues. He had never been arrested, never committed a violent crime, and his marks were almost always big companies covered by insurance. He never stole from the little guy. He did, however, run a small stable of girls for a while.

At the time I met Willie, the life on the streets was in a period of transition. The gang bangers had moved in and even the old pros like Willie wanted no part of that action.

After purchasing the ceiling fans Willie had in his trunk, he wanted to know if I needed any help installing them. Coincidently, I was currently between maintenance men so I hired Willie to do the work. He has been with me ever since. He has been my right hand man. I couldn't have operated my rentals without him. He could fix most anything mechanical, knew how to handle tools, and from his B&E days he had developed the skill of lock picking. That came in handy when a belligerent tenant changed a lock and wouldn't share a key.

When I retired and sold the apartments, he retired too. He lives in the small efficiency unit in my basement. He's got his little shop and gets his rent free for taking care of my remaining two buildings.

Willie didn't have much schooling, but he is street smart. He could con with the best of them. His best act is to play the part of the good ole boy Negro that is usually depicted in movies of the prewar era. He could be Kingfish from Amos 'n Andy, Stepnfetchit, or a character right out of Uncle Remus.

On more than one occasion I've heard him lament, "These damn kids today don't how to do no con. They thinks they all cool with their cornrows and dreadlocks and shit stickin' outta dere face. They ain't gonna con no white dude with all that shit. They just gonna scare the bejesus out of 'em and they gonna call the cops. You wanna con a white dude you gotta get their confidence. Ain't no white dude gonna trust these young punks."

And he was right.

Willie could be a black me. I was just a year older than Willie, we both had a slender build, and we both were as grey headed as could be. There was, however, one significant difference. Willie was hung like a horse. He had a schlong that would be the envy of John Holmes and, well, you remember my situation with Nurse Ratchet. Not in the same ballpark, so to speak.

One day when we were feeling particularly chummy, I said, "Willie, we're about the same age. How come you're not starting to shrivel up like me?"

"Exercise, Mr. Walt. You got a muscle you want to beef up, you gotta give it plenty of exercise. The mo' the betta. You know de ole sayin', use it or lose it!"

AHHH, so that's the problem.

Willie probably had never heard of Confucius, but he certainly had lived his life according to one of his dictates: "Foolish man give wife grand piano, wise man give wife upright organ."

As I came up the sidewalk Willie waved, "Evenin' Mr. Walt," he said.

"How are you doing today Willie?" I replied.

"Well," he stammered, "not doin' too good today. I kinda got me a personal problem."

"Exactly what kind of personal problem?" I asked, figuring he needed to borrow some money until his social security check arrived.

"Well, it's like dis. I had me a date with Emma yesterday and I was all lookin' forward to it, but something didn't feel quite right, you know, down dere," and he pointed to his crotch. "You know, it's kinda like when you got a six cylinder car and it's only hittin' on four cylinders. It's needin' a tune-up. I didn't want to disappoint Emma. I got a reputation to protect, you know. So I figured I'd get me a tune-up. Bought me some of that Vi-agra stuff from Benny down on 12th street. He said it was real good shit. So, I took it and sho' enough, it WAS good shit. Problem is the directions said if yo' erection lasts longer dan fo' hours, you betta see yo' doc."

"So," I asked, "did your erection last four hours?"

"Hell yes, it lasted fo' hours. Hell, I was with Emma fo' hours. Like to killed the po' girl. When she couldn't take no mo' I came on home but it still wouldn't go away. Shit, man, I been stiff so long, I been pissing on my bathroom wall!"

"I was beginnin' to get concerned so I took mysef down to Doc Buleah's free clinic. She's real discreet, you know. That woman took one look at my problem, said 'OH WILLIE!' and jumped my old bones right there on the exam table."

"Well, did that take care of the problem?" I asked.

"Hell no," he replied.

"Have you tried taking a cold shower?" I asked.

"Yep, I had me one of them, too. Only thing I got outta dat was a really good place to hang my soap-on-a-rope."

I hadn't noticed that the Professor had been sitting quietly on the porch swing listening to our conversation. He rose, walked over, and simply said, "Think a thought that's iffy and you'll lose your stiffy," and he went inside.

"What de hell dat ole man talkin' about?" Willie asked.

"Gosh Willie," I said. "I think what you need is a distraction. Something to take your mind off your---you know what."

Just then, old Mrs. Bassett from 1-A came out the door. She's eighty-five, wrinkled as a prune, her boobs hang down to her waist and she has a big hairy mole on her lower lip. But she's really sweet. As she walked by I whispered in Willie's ear, "How'd you like to have a piece of that?"

"Oh God," he screamed, "don't even say dat. Ohhhhh---dat's one picture I can't get outta my mind and----and----." Then he looked down, felt his crotch and a big grin spread across his face. "You done did it," he exclaimed. "It's gone! I knew I could count on you, Mr. Walt. Well I better go see if Emma's OK."

And off he went.

CHAPTER 7

I'M CERTAINLY NOT IN Willie's league, but I do have a lady friend. Her name is Margaret McBride. I call her Maggie. We worked together at the real estate office before I retired.

Besides being my sweetie, she was also my main competition at the office. She is a spunky gal of Irish ancestry with fiery red hair and a personality to match. She is my age but just not quite ready to hang up the old briefcase. She really enjoys her work and the pay is pretty darn good for a 66 year old.

The reason our relationship works is that we both understand the demands of our profession. Realtors and cops have a lot in common. Both professions have activities and schedules that a normal person just doesn't understand unless they've been there and done that. In fact, realtors and cops are among the professions with the highest divorce rate. Hmmmm.

If only guys would pay attention to the wisdom of the Old Masters. I heard the Professor once say: "Man who fight with girlfriend all day get no piece at night."

Sage advice!

We enjoy doing things together. We both like movies, the theatre, dancing and eating out.

Neither of us are big drinkers. We have friends who are and I've discovered that alcohol consumption is a world of its own.

I enjoy an occasional Margarita. I have friends who will order one too and specify "Gold Tequila, top shelf." What's that all about? What difference does it make what color it is? When they mix it with the other stuff, it always comes out green anyway. And who cares what shelf they keep in on?

We also occasionally enjoy a glass of wine with our evening meal. Boy! Don't get me started on wine. What's the deal with the cork? I hate corks. First, if you finally manage to get the damn thing out and don't drink the whole bottle, the sucker will never go back in. You have to get out your picket knife and whittle the damn thing. Ever try to whittle a cork? It's not pretty.

I'm fairly mechanical. I can hold my own with power tools, but I've never been able to master the corkscrew. No matter what I do, the top of the cork comes out stuck in the screw and the other half is an inch below the lip of the bottle. Nothing spoils the mood of the evening more than having to get out the old Black & Decker and drill out the rest of the cork. Give me a screw top bottle any day.

I just don't understand pairings. You know, red wine with beef, white wine with fish and on and on and on. In my humble opinion, if it's a good wine it will taste good with anything.

And the price! Wow! I had a client give me a bottle of Dom Perignon. He said it cost him 150 bucks. I thought, "Man, this is going to be really good." It tasted like Heinz vinegar.

My personal favorite is Arbor Mist. It comes with a screw cap. You can get it in six different flavors and it only costs $3.59 a bottle. Just $3.29 if you catch it on sale. And, it tastes good with everything. My flavor of choice is Peach Chardonnay. It goes great with tuna casserole, my signature dish.

Maggie and I really enjoy our time together. I would categorize our intimate moments more as playful than erotic. No rough stuff.

I recall one evening. We had just enjoyed a wonderful tuna casserole topped off with a flute of Arbor Mist. See, I told you. We were both feeling pretty mellow, but I could see Maggie was distracted.

"What's on your mind?" I asked.

"Business has been a little slow the past few days and I just feel guilty being here and not out showing property," she replied.

"Well," I said, "if you're determined to wear your realtor hat this evening, how about me being your client? I'm sure you have some things I might want to see."

"What exactly are you looking for?" she asked.

"Something warm and comfortable and fairly easy to get into." I replied.

She grinned and I knew she was getting the hint. "I think I might have just the thing for you," she said. "It has a nice firm foundation and there are a pair of balconies on the second floor that overlook two beautiful blue pools."

"Wow, sounds great," I said, "How do I go about getting in?"

"Whoa! Not so fast, Buster," she said. "I have to prequalify you before I can let you in. What kind of down payment are you talking about here?"

"Well, I don't have a HUGE down payment, but what I have is HARD cash. And I believe my ASSets are sufficient to meet your needs."

With that, she slipped off her top. "Well, how do you like the view so far!" she asked.

"Not bad." I replied. "Lovely view of the mountains from here."

"Then are you ready to make an offer?" she asked.

"Not quite," I replied. "What kind of buyer would I be if I didn't do my due-diligence? I never make an offer without a whole house inspection. And I must warn you, my inspections are VERY thorough."

"And it's my duty as your agent to inform you of any issues you should be aware of," she replied. "In the interest of full disclosure, I have to tell you there's definitely moisture in the basement."

With that encouragement, I slid my hand up her skirt. "Ah yes," I said. "Definitely moist, but I don't think this will be a deal breaker."

She suddenly drew back. "Have you thought about insurance?" she asked.

"I believe I'm fully covered," I replied.

"Well, I think we may be ready to move forward," she said.

"First, I need to know if there's a warranty with this transaction," I stated.

"Oh yeah," she replied, "I guarantee you will be completely satisfied!"

Later that night we closed escrow.

After my eventful first day on the job, I was ready to kick back and just chill for the evening. But the phone rang.

"Evening, Walt, this is Mary. Old Mr. Feeny in #14 stopped up the toilet again. You better send Willie over with the plunger."

"Swell," I replied. "What in the world does that old man eat?"

"I haven't the faintest," she said. "But when he's ready to pass it, I wish he'd take it down to the Quick Trip on the corner. They got one of them vacuum flushers. It'll damn near suck your ass down the toilet if you ain't careful."

Mary Murphy is the resident manager in my only other building, The Three Trails Hotel. When I sold all my rentals to the young couple, they refused to take this property. I don't blame them. This property is a lot like most women.

High maintenance.

In the 1800's, Kansas City was the last major outpost on the way west. The Oregon, California and Santa Fe Trails originated from the Westport area. My hotel was built way back then. Hence, the name, Three Trails. It was a grand hotel back in the day. But as the property changed hands over the years, so did its' use and condition. It was even a brothel for a while. When I purchased it, it was a flophouse for druggies, crack heads and various other human vermin. I evicted everyone, remodeled the building and made it a respectable flophouse.

It consists of 20 single rooms, each with a bed, dresser and chair, 4 full bathrooms and a small apartment for the Manager. You do the math. We just hope all 20 tenants don't get the squirts at the same time.

My tenants are mostly old retired men and single guys that work out of the labor pool. Pay by the week. $40.00 cash. Bookkeeping nightmare. That's why I have Mary.

Mary is a young, sturdy 75 year old who carries a Hillrich & Bradsby white ash baseball bat and she doesn't take any crap off anyone. Including me. If she had been a man, she probably would have been Harmon Killebrew. Some people just have an aura about them that says, "If you mess with me, sucker, I'll split your skull." Mary has that aura.

More than once I've heard her bellow, "LENNY, YOU SHITHEAD! You pissed on the floor again. Now get your ass in there and clean it up!!!"

"Yes, Ma'am."

Mary is my resident Manager. She gets her rent free for keeping the boys in line. If she ever left me, I'd have to burn down the Hotel.

CHAPTER 8

I AWOKE BEFORE THE ALARM went off the next morning, eager to begin my second day in my new career. It's amazing to what degree our minds control our bodies. For the past year or so, I had been lethargic and bored and my life was seemingly pointed in no particular direction. It didn't really matter whether I drug myself out of bed at 7:00 or at 9:00. I can truly understand why so many men suddenly die soon after retirement.

Today was different. I awoke revitalized. I have a purpose, a destiny to fulfill. After all, I'm now Lady Justice's newest recruit in the never-ending battle to balance the scales of life. To protect the young, the weak, the innocent from those that would do harm and make them accountable for their evil deeds. Kind of like my childhood hero, from mild man and reporter to the nemesis of evildoers, and here am I, from mild man and realtor to the newest champion of justice.

Wow! Who wouldn't be excited?

I gathered in the squad room along with the regular officers, poured myself a cup of the black sludge that impersonates coffee at the precinct. I was eagerly awaiting the arrival of Captain Short for our morning briefing when I was bumped from behind, spilling the black goo down the front of my clean uniform shirt.

"Oh sorry, Grandpa, I didn't see you sitting there," quipped Murdock as he snickered and looked around the room for approval. "I heard you were a real hero yesterday. First day on the job and all. Must have been beginner's luck. Just a word of warning. You're not a cop. You're a civilian and an old one at that. I don't know what they were thinking, bringing you guys in here. I'm warning you. Just stay out of my way."

At that moment, a large hand grabbed Murdock by the collar and lifted him till he was standing on his tiptoes.

"Morning Murdock," Ox said. "I see you've met my new partner. Hell of a guy. Saved my ass yesterday. From now on, you got anything to say to him, you're saying it to both of us. You get the picture?" And he let go of Murdock who slipped on the coffee he had caused me to spill and sat down flat on his butt. A muffled snicker was heard circulating around the room.

Good job Lady Justice. We're on the same page.

Ox sat down next to me and said, "Good morning, Walt. Everything OK?"

"What the hell was that all about?" I asked. "What did I ever do to that guy?"

"Well for starters, the guy is just an asshole," Ox replied. "Most of the other guys avoid him cause he's always starting trouble and getting in somebody's face. On top of that, you shocked the shit out of his old friend Captain Harrington. I don't think you're gonna be on either one of their Christmas card lists."

At that moment, Captain Short entered the room.

"At ease, men," Shorty barked. "Our first order of business today is to congratulate Office George Wilson and his new partner Walter Williams for the apprehension of the Livestock Exchange thieves. Good job, guys."

A round of applause circulated around the room. Except for Murdock. He was sitting in the back of the room and you could almost see the steam rising from the top of his head.

"We've got a problem," Shorty continued. "We've had a string of hit and run assaults in Gillham Park. A white male, about 5 feet 10 inches, 175 pounds, dressed in a black hooded sweatshirt has been hiding in the shrubbery waiting for an easy mark to pass by. He runs out, strikes the victim so fast they don't know what hit them, and runs away with their purses."

"We've got witnesses, but at the time of day he strikes, the only people in the park are moms or nannies with their kids or senior citizens out for a stroll. Certainly no one who could fight back. He's obviously cased the park and knows when it's easy pickings. By the time someone calls 911 and we respond, the perp's long gone."

"We've tried staking out the park, but the perp never attacks when our guys are around. I think any viable male in the area discourages him and he has the luxury of picking his time and place. We don't have the manpower to stake out the park 24/7. Any ideas?"

Everyone looked anxiously around the room waiting for someone to come up with a plan. No one spoke.

"Hmmm," I thought. "Senior citizens and nannies!" And an idea began to form in my head. I was reluctant to speak up, being the new guy and all, but then I thought, "What the hell. There's a time to be mild mannered and a time for action."

"Uhhhh, Captain Short," I said. And raised my hand like I was back in second grade.

"Yes, Williams," the Captain acknowledged.

"Well, Captain, I know I'm the new guy here, but I do have an idea," I stammered.

Lots of sideways glances and eye rolling from the other officers.

"Let's hear it," barked the captain.

"Sir, you mentioned that regular officers seem to scare the perp away, but senior citizens don't seem to be a threat. What if you had a senior citizen planted in the park with a wire?" I pointed to my head of grey hair and said, "You could place a backup officer close by, but out of sight. If the perp showed up I could immediately call for backup and keep an eye on the perp until help arrived."

The Captain thought for a moment. "It has some possibilities," he said. "You and Ox please hang around for a minute. The rest of you men are dismissed to your regular assignments."

When everyone was gone but us, the Captain spoke up. "Walt, I like your idea. Nothing else has worked so far and we're getting a lot of pressure from citizens. They're afraid to go into the park. But I am concerned about deliberately putting a civilian, even if you are CPP, in harm's way."

"Not to worry, Captain," I said. "Obviously the perp doesn't consider old guys, like me, to be a threat. In fact, nobody really pays much attention to seniors. It's like we're invisible. We just kind of blend into the background. And anyway, I probably won't be anywhere near the perp when he strikes. It's a big park."

"All right," the Captain replied. "Ox, take Walt down and get him fitted for a wire. You'll need to go home and change into civilian clothing. And give me a call when you're set up in the park."

"Aye, Aye, Captain," I said, "I'll go home get on my best brown plaid polyester pants and suspenders."

When I arrived home, Willie was sitting on the front steps.

"Jesus, Mr. Walt," he exclaimed. "You gotta get rid of that old man Feeny in #14. That guy must eat buzzard puke for dinner. I ain't never smelled nothin' like that befo'. Anyway, what you doin' home this time o' day? I thought you be out fightin' crime."

So I told him about the sitting in the park.

Without hesitation, Willie's street experience on the other side of the law kicked into gear.

"What you need is a sidekick," he said. "You gonna need some help. What you gonna do all day. Jus' sit dere wif you' finger up you' ass? If this perp has any brains at all, he gonna be watchin' who's comin' and goin'. If somethin' don't look right, he ain't gonna show. Now jus' think about it. Two grizzled old farts sitting at a picnic table playing checkers. Fits right in. Dey could sit dere fo' hours and nobody would notice. Besides, I got me a prop."

And he disappeared into the building. He came back holding a walking cane with a shiny brass handle at the top. "A rich guy sorta gave me this one night when I was in his house. I know someday it would come in handy." He grinned.

So off we went to meet Ox.

"Oh man," he said as Willie and I walked up. "The Captain's gonna shit a brick. He was worried about one civilian. Now we got two."

"That's one BIG mothafucker," Willie whispered in my ear.

I introduced my two friends, shared some of Willie's background with Ox and promoted our checker idea. Reluctantly, he agreed.

We found our picnic table in the middle of the park where we had a good view of both ends. Ox parked his car two blocks away from the park in the lot of a convenience store. He was maybe two minutes away. We set up our checkerboard and the sting was on.

There weren't many people in the park. The word had gotten around and scared citizens were probably steering clear till the robber was caught.

An older, large black woman was pushing a stroller with a white baby. Probably a nanny. An old man in ratty clothing with a bottle wrapped in a brown paper bag was stretched out on a bench, asleep, and two boys about eight to ten years old were riding their bikes on the asphalt around the playground. Peaceful.

No action. About noon, a young woman appeared from the direction of the parking lot. She had a Burger King bag in one hand and a large purse slung over her shoulder. Probably a secretary escaping from the madhouse in her office for a peaceful lunch in the park.

The moment she laid her purse on the table, a man in a hooded sweatshirt emerged from the bushes close by. As he approached, the woman screamed and grabbed for her purse, but it was too late. The perp grabbed the purse and took off.

"Ox, we got him," I yelled into the wire, "get over here, quick!"

"On the way," he replied.

Fortunately, the perp was running in Ox's direction. Since there was only one vehicle entrance into the park, we were worried he might escape in another direction, but he must have had a vehicle close by in the parking lot.

Ox came screaming around the corner, lights and sirens blaring on the black and white. The perp came to a sudden stop. He was cutoff from his means of escape. He furtively glanced around the park and spied the young boys riding their bikes. He sprinted over to them, knocked the boy off of the biggest bike, slung the purse over his shoulder and took off pedaling down the path that would take him right by our picnic table.

As he was approaching, Willie leaped to his feet with the timing and grace of a fencing master, and as the bike passed he thrust the cane into the whirling spokes. The bike came to a sudden screeching halt. The perp was catapulted over the handlebars as if he had been shot out of a cannon. He flew a good ten feet in the air and landed with a dull thud.

It's funny what pops into your mind during times of stress, but there it was, thanks to the Professor and his Muse:

"Man who fly upside down have big crack up."

Go figure.

"All right, we got him," I exclaimed as I rushed toward him with cuffs ready. But just as I was in reach, he pulled himself to his feet and took off on the run.

Now I'm no slouch when it comes to running. When I was a kid, I discovered you've gotta be fast when you only weigh 120 pounds, but I soon discovered I had lost a little something in the last 40 years. This kid, about a third my age, was gaining ground on me fast. I did a quick mental calculation, remembering that my taser wires had a range of 15 feet. I knew I had one shot. I whipped out my Benford #5 on the run, pointed and fired. I saw the probes leap forward and bury themselves firmly in the perp's butt cheeks. He went rigid, then limp, and hit the ground face first with a sickening thud.

I rushed up to extract the taser probes and I noticed his ass was quivering like a bowl of Jell-O.

COOL!

I cuffed his hands behind his back and rolled him over. His hood dropped away. I saw his face for the first time and realized this was the kid that tackled the old lady in the Price Chopper Supermarket parking lot and had initiated my quest to become a cop.

Sweet Justice!!

Willie rushed up to me, took a look at the perp writhing on the ground, and a big grin spread across his face and we gave each other a high five.

The 'Over The Hill Gang' rides again!!

We dropped Willie off at the apartment then took the perp to the station and booked him in. We decided it might be best to not mention Willie to Captain Short.

When I got home that evening, Willie was again waiting for me on the front steps. He had a plastic bag from the 'Shirt Shop' on his lap. He proudly handed me the bag. I pulled out two shirts with these words emblazoned in bold red letters..........

"OLD GUYS RULE!"

"Oh, Lord, what have I done?"

CHAPTER 9

THE NEXT MORNING at roll call Captain Short congratulated us for the second day in a row. With the apprehension of the Gillham Park Mugger, word had spread through the precinct that Ox and I had made two good busts in two days. We were now being playfully dubbed, 'The Dynamic Duo.'

Swell.

Then the Captain got serious. A 42-year-old real estate agent, Nancy Duncan, had gone missing from an open house she was holding. The sellers had returned home, found the door ajar and signs of a struggle, but no Nancy. Her car was found locked on the street in front of the house. This had all the earmarks of abduction. A yellow alert had been issued and photos of Nancy were passed among the officers.

I knew Nancy from my real estate days. She was a 15-year veteran and a real pro. She knew her business.

You need to understand some characteristics of the women in the real estate business. I do. I worked beside them for 30 years.

There's an old joke that has been floating around real estate offices for as long as I can remember;

Question: What's the difference between a pit bull and a lady realtor?

Answer: Lip gloss.

Get the picture?

While women in many other fields have bumped up against the 'glass ceiling' of corporate America, and female college graduates are struggling as secretaries and bookkeepers at minimum wage, a good female realtor in a hot market can bring in a six figure income easily. At any real estate company in any market, the majority of top producers are women.

They have big incomes, big cars, and big egos to match. One of my pet peeves is that these gals, many of whom are excellent salespersons, would come in second place in a one-person beauty contest. Yet, they go to Glamour Shots photo studio, get a pound of makeup plastered to their face and a hairdo that they will never wear again, and put that photo on their business cards. Sheesh, talk about truth in advertising. One evening, when railing to the Professor about one particular lady he replied: "Women who wear wonder bra make mountains out of molehills."

What a guy!

These women are determined. Realtor income is commission only. You don't work, you don't get paid. It's a very motivating principle. Consequently, there's inevitable competition among agents for clients. While most agents get along fine, some of these gals are ruthless.

Maggie is, of course, a realtor. She's good. She works hard and her clients love her. The picture on her business card is really Maggie. But she does have a bit of that bulldog deep inside. I've seen her deal with another agent who was trying to steal one of her clients. By the time she was through with him, he thought he had two assholes, because she's just ripped him a new one. You really don't want to piss off that little Irish redhead.

"MAGGIE!"

Oh my God! I've got to give her a heads up. I called her cell and she picked up on the second ring.

"Maggie, have you heard......?"

"Yes," she interrupted. Our Broker just called a sales meeting to let everyone know that Nancy's missing. The Board of Realtors has issued an alert. They have asked all agents to take extreme caution. Don't meet new clients at vacant houses. Try to avoid open houses and make sure our cans of pepper spray are still active. We're all scared to death."

"Sounds like good advice," I replied. "You be careful. I don't want to lose you."

"See you tonight," she said and hung up.

Just as the Captain was ready to dismiss the squad meeting, an officer came in with a sheet of paper. "You'd better take a look at this, Captain," he said.

The Captain studied the paper for several minutes. "Gentlemen," he said, "I'm afraid I have some bad news. Nancy Duncan's nude body was found floating in Loose Park Lake this morning. There were ligature marks around her feet, wrists and neck and preliminary reports indicate she was sexually assaulted with some large object. There was a plastic sandwich bag attached to her stomach with duct tape. Inside the bag was one of Ms. Duncan's full-page ads with the headline, 'Two Million Dollar Producer'. A note, with letters obviously cut from a magazine, read, 'She was worth every penny of it.' "

We all sat in stunned silence. While murder is not an everyday occurrence at the station, most mayhem is one gang banger killing a rival gang member or a drug deal gone bad. But when it happens to a respected, successful person like Nancy, it really hits close to home. It makes you realize no one is truly immune from violence and that all of us are just a random violent act away from death.

Where is the justice in this?

We solemnly went about our patrol duties wondering if this was just a random act or, God forbid, just the opening act of a serial killer. There was no joy in Mudville that day. A vicious killer had lashed out.

After work I went straight to Maggie's apartment. Upon entering, I found her curled up on the couch, a half empty box of Kleenex in her lap. Her eyes were red and swollen.

Without a word I sat down on the couch beside her. "I served with Nancy on the Professional Standards Committee," was all she said, and then sobbed uncontrollably. I held her for a long time that night.

CHAPTER 10

THE NEXT MORNING I was totally distracted by the previous day's events. My heart ached for Maggie and for Nancy and I was so pissed that one person could create so much heartache in so many lives.

At squad meeting we were told that at this time there were no suspects in the murder. No clues were found around the lake and no witnesses had come forward. The autopsy was not yet completed. Damn!

Ox and I were on our regular patrol when a message came over the two-way radio. "Assault in progress at 507 Linwood Boulevard. Any officers in the area please respond."

"Car 54 on route," Ox replied, "ETA 10 minutes."

As Ox sped away that address hit me between my eyes like a ton of bricks. "That's my Three Trails Hotel," I shouted. "Move it!"

We pulled up in front of the Hotel. A crowd had gathered and was staring at the front porch roof. A skanky looking white guy was cowering in the corner of the porch roof. Big Mary was standing over him with her Hillrich & Bradsby. We got there just in time to hear her say, "Go ahead, Punk. Make my day!"

"Jesus," I thought, "Dirty Mary! She's been watching those Clint Eastwood movies again."

"Get her away from me, PLEASE!" the skanky guy shouted.

"Shut up or I'll knock your skinny white ass clear over to Main Street," she shouted back.

"Mary," I called.

She looked down, saw me, and a big grin spread across her face. "Hey, Mr. Walt," she exclaimed, "I got me a squatter."

The skanky guy, who couldn't have weighed more than 110 pounds, seeing her momentarily distracted, decided to make a break for it. Mary was standing between him and the window so he barreled into her. 'WHUMP!' Mary was planted like an oak. All 200 pounds of her. After the initial impact, he kind of slid down the front of her body like Wile E. Coyote does when he hits a rock wall.

"I'll teach you not to squat in my hotel," she said, and kicked him in the ribs.

It turned out that the guy was coming in at night after everyone was asleep and locking himself in one of the shared hall baths. If a tenant got up to use the can and found the door locked, he just assumed it was another tenant answering a nocturnal call of nature and he simply went to another bathroom. The guy made sure he was out by the time the tenants were rising.

Mary had found some needles and a white powder in the bathroom the day before. She feared one of our regular tenants was using drugs, so she decided to stake out the bathroom. Finding it locked, she gathered her bat, a pillow and blanket and quietly camped outside the bathroom door.

Imagine the surprise of Mr. Squatter when he opened the door only to be nose to nose with Dirty Mary.

We cuffed and frisked the guy and found a bag of crack cocaine in his pocket.

Sweet!

You think this guy will tell his grandkids about the day he got his ass kicked by a 75-year-old senior citizen with a 36-inch bat? Probably not! But it's justice!

That evening on the way home I stopped by the Shirt Shop. Now Mary has a T-shirt that says:

"OLD GALS RULE!"

CHAPTER 11

IT SEEMS THAT CRIME never takes a holiday. Even though our thoughts were focused on the murder of Nancy Duncan, other victims deserved our attention as well.

Downtown Kansas City had recently been the scene of a series of 'snatch and grabs' at ATM machines. Downtown Kansas City from 9th Street on the north to 12th Street on the south and Oak Street on the east to Main Street on the west is a labyrinth of multi-storied office and retail buildings, including the famous 'Petticoat Lane.' Running between each block is an alley that provides access to loading docks and service entrances. Several large national banks have branches in this area with ATM machines in front at sidewalk level for the convenience of their patrons.

In this most recent crime spree, patrons who had just withdrawn cash from the ATMs were suddenly rushed by a very fleet-of-foot young Latino boy who snatched the cash from their hands and dashed away and disappeared into the back alleys.

Ox and I had been assigned to patrol the area on foot. The ultimate goal was to catch the kid in the act, but at the very least, to give the citizens a sense of security. The target area was twelve square blocks with four ATM machines scattered throughout. We decided to split up, keeping in touch at regular intervals with our walkie-talkies.

As I walked the sidewalks of Downtown Kansas City, I was struck by the diversity of the people who mingled there on a daily basis. Prominent were the businessmen and women. Even on scorcher days such as this one, they dressed in suits and ties and pantsuits. These were the movers and shakers of Kansas City commerce and industry, on their way to their air-conditioned offices high above the city street.

The postman, the UPS driver, laborers and deliverymen all scurried about at the bidding of the suits. Women with shopping bags went window to window searching for the next bargain. Vendors on the street sold newspapers and hot dogs and at the corner of an alley was an old woman in a long coat carrying all her worldly possessions in a shopping cart. All men are created equal. They just don't stay that way for very long.

I strolled by the first ATM. A line had formed behind the woman at the machine and those waiting behind her appeared to be agitated. As I approached, I saw her hit the machine with her fist and mutter, "That sonofabitch! He took out all the cash. Just wait till I get a hold of him tonight."

Oh-Oh, somebody's in trouble. She gave the machine a kick. Right! Like it was the machine's fault. She retrieved her card and huffed away. A round of applause arose from the queue behind her. She turned and gave them the finger.

Happy Days!

The M.O. of the grabber had been to hit single individuals. Not so many witnesses and less chance for there to be a hero close by.

I crossed the street and wandered into the next block toward the second ATM. A middle-aged man in a business suit was just keying in his pin number when I saw a Latino boy about thirteen or fourteen years old come strolling up the sidewalk. He obviously had practiced his approach. His timing was perfect. He came even with the man just as the machine spewed out a handful of bills. With the speed of a striking snake, he dashed up, reached in front of the man, snatched the cash and sped away.

I keyed the mike, "I got him, Ox, alley, 10th and Grand." And I took off after him. There wasn't a chance in hell that a sixty-five year old man could outrun a fourteen-year old kid. My goal was to follow close enough so that I could see where he was disappearing to after each grab.

I was maybe fifty feet behind him when I saw him duck down the alley. It took maybe all of fifteen seconds for me to reach the corner and charge into the alley after him. I raced around the corner and had advanced twenty feet into the alley when I spotted the kid. He was right in front of me, standing perfectly still. And right behind him was a Latino man, maybe thirty-five years old with a .380 pointed right at my head.

I came to an abrupt halt and two more Latino guys in their late teens moved in behind me and grabbed my arms. After I was pinned, the guy stuck his gun in his pants and advanced toward me. Without so much as a word, he struck me squarely in the stomach. I groaned, bent forward and gasped for air. He came at me again with an uppercut, snapping my head back. My lights went out and as I was going down, I heard Ox pounding around the corner.

"Es el gordo!" snapped the Latino. "Vamanos." They dropped me and disappeared down the alley.

As I regained consciousness, I was aware of Ox and two paramedics hovered over me.

"He's coming around," I heard one of the medics say. "Let's try to get you up."

My ribs hurt like hell and I noticed blood was on my shirt from my swollen lip. "Did you get 'em?" I asked.

"No," Ox replied, "I stayed with you till the medics and backup got here. They got away."

Swell! Beat up for nothing.

The medics insisted I go to the hospital for x-rays on the ribs and to be checked for a concussion. After a thorough exam, I was told I would probably live, and was dismissed. The way I felt, I wasn't sure I agreed with them.

I took the rest of the day off and as I drove home, wincing in pain with every breath, I began to question what the hell I thought I was doing.

"Christ, Walt," I said to myself. "You're sixty-five years old. You're supposed to be playing golf and fishing and traveling. What in the world were you thinking?"

And I remembered another time I felt this way. I was fifteen years old and I had just been run over by a two hundred and fifty pound defensive tackle. What lesson did I learn from that? I quit football. I had just been mugged by a Latino tough guy with a .380. Is there a message here? The more I drove, the more I hurt and the more discouraged I became.

I arrived at my apartment and as I was going in the door, I was met by the Professor. "Good Lord, Walt!" he exclaimed. "You look like crap. What happened?"

Nice of you to notice!

I went into the Professor's apartment, dropped in a chair and spilled my guts about my beating and my self doubts. The Professor just sat quietly as I indulged in my pity party.

He offered no sympathy or advice or admonitions. He just listened. When I had finished with my rantings, he slowly rose and went to his desk. He returned with a piece of paper, and as he handed it to me he said,

"Why don't you go upstairs, take a long hot shower, pour a glass of Arbor Mist and think about this before you make any decisions."

So I did. I stood in the shower with scalding water pouring over me until it turned cold. I poured a glass of Peach Chardonnay, sat down and read the words on the paper he had given me.

> When things go wrong, as they sometimes will
> When the road you're trudging seems all uphill
> When care is pressing you down a bit
> Rest, if you must, but don't you quit.
> Life is queer with its twists and turns
> As everyone of us sometimes learns
> And many a failure turns about
> When he might have won if he stuck it out.
> Don't give up though the pace seems slow-
> You may succeed with another blow.
> Success is failure turned inside out-
> The silver tint of the clouds of doubt.
> And you never can tell how close you are.
> It may be near when it seems so far.
> So stick to the fight when you're hardest hit-
> It's when things seem worst that you must not QUIT!

That's not what I wanted to hear! I wanted someone to say, "Oh, poor Walt. Give up this nonsense and just go back to being plain old you." But I didn't like that guy anymore.

Then I thought of my own heroes. No matter how badly they were beaten, did Roy and Gene ever throw in the towel? I don't think so. And even Superman had kryptonite to contend with. Life is full of adversity. You can either bow to it or stand up to it.

Then another thought struck me. I don't play golf! I never have. And fish smell really bad. And who wants to travel alone? Maybe I'll stick it out a while longer.

I called the Professor and thanked him and went to bed.

When I crawled out of bed the next morning, I had the distinct feeling I had been hit by a semi. I looked in the mirror at my bruised and swollen lip. The Red Badge of Courage. Right? I figured the best way to take my mind off my aches and pains was to get my ass in gear, get to work and figure how to catch these guys.

In the squad room, Ox, the Captain and I reviewed the data we had. At least my confrontation had revealed that the kid wasn't acting alone. In fact, it seemed like the story out of <u>Oliver Twist</u> where Fagan was sending the kids into the streets to do his dirty work. We had come close to nabbing them, but we obviously needed more reinforcements. One patrolman didn't stand a chance against four armed Latinos. Unfortunately with the recent murder, manpower was spread thin. We decided to continue our foot patrol, but not split up as before.

We walked the streets as briskly as possible trying to cover the ground between the four ATM machines, but it was impossible to be everywhere at once. We were a block away when the kid struck that morning. By the time we arrived on the scene there was no sign of the grabber. According to witnesses, he had ducked down another alley and disappeared. We checked the alley looking for any sign of the perps but only found a UPS truck and a van with Moonlight Maintenance on the side. Just normal people doing their normal jobs.

I had a thought. These guys obviously have a foolproof way of disappearing after the grab. We don't have a clue where to look for them. What if we could plant a tracking device in the money they grab, let them make their getaway and then follow them to their hideout. We couldn't put tracking devices on all the money coming out of every machine, but if we had a uniform standing close by three of the machines, they would be forced to hit the fourth machine. We needed a plant. Someone non threatening, who could watch until there was no line at the machine and then go to make a withdrawal. But the cash would actually already be in hand and fixed with a tracking device.

Hmmmmm. Mary!

I shared my idea with Ox and the Captain. The Captain was reluctant at first, but I reminded him that no one had been injured, just scared, and he finally agreed.

That afternoon I went to the Three Trails and told Mary my idea. "What do you think?" I asked. "Are you in?"

"Hell yes, I'm in!" she declared. "It's been too damn quiet around here lately. I've been bored. I need to kick some ass!"

"No ass kicking." I replied. But I wasn't too worried. I remembered how fast the kid was, and while Mary is tough, she's not that mobile.

The next morning, Ox was staked out at one ATM in full dress uniform, I was at another and a third officer covered the other machine. Mary was in a coffee shop across from the fourth ATM. She was to watch and wait until there was no line, then approach the machine and act as if she were making a withdrawal, but the money with the device would already be in her hand. If there was no attempt, she was to return to the coffee shop, wait thirty minutes and repeat the process.

She made her first withdrawal without incident and returned to the coffee shop. A half hour later she tried again. This time the kid came out of nowhere grabbed the money from her hand and sped away. "Git back here you little shit!" she screamed, but the kid was long gone.

So far, so good.

This time, we made no attempt to apprehend. We wanted to follow them to their safe house. The third officer took Mary home while Ox and I tracked the little green blip on the screen in the squad car.

It was no surprise that the blip was leading us to Kansas City's west side. There is a large Latino community there. After about twenty minutes, the blip became stationery and we knew they had reached their destination.

We slowly cruised the neighborhood and when we were within a block we stopped and surveyed the street. And there it was! It had been right in front of us all along. A panel truck with Moonlight Maintenance on the side. Trucks of all sizes and shapes are supposed to be in alleys. That's what they do. Nothing suspicious there. They were hiding in plain sight. After the cops leave the alley, they just drive away.

Pretty slick!

Ox and I had done our job. The perps were in the house with the marked money. It was time to turn the situation over to the tough guys. We called it in and soon officers with helmets, shields, a battering ram and big guns were on the scene.

Ox watched the front and I was stationed in the back as the assault team got into position.

I heard a loud 'crash' and shouting as the team breeched the doorway. After the initial assault, it became quiet and I assumed the bad guys were being cuffed and Mirandized.

Then I saw a basement window slide open and the Latino, who had knocked me on my kiester, was crawling out.

I was fifty yards away from him and, again, figured that the chances of my sixty-five year old legs catching him were slim.

He hadn't noticed me as he took off across the lawn toward a park and ball field on the next corner.

I quickly searched my mental database of useless information and pulled out a postulate I had learned in high school geometry. The hypotenuse of a right triangle is longer than it's sides, or something like that. Basically, I had the angle on him and if I got my butt in gear, I could cut him off at the park.

See kids, you may actually use that math stuff someday.

I took off and raced toward the ball field where a group of neighborhood kids were playing ball. I drew my revolver and assumed the two-hand stance just like I remembered Sergeant Joe Friday do it.

The perp hadn't seen me yet and as he approached, I pointed directly at him and yelled, "FREEZE! POLICE!"

He looked up startled, and instead of stopping, raising his hands and surrendering like he was supposed to, he grabbed the closest kid. How come these guys can't follow a script?

He had grabbed the catcher, a portly kid decked out in shin guards, chest protector and helmet. He pulled his .380 and held it against the kid's helmet. "Drop it copper," he said, "or I'll put one right in this kid's head."

I hesitated only a moment as I saw the look of terror in the boy's face. As I slowly knelt and placed my gun on the ground, the perp started backing away, putting distance between us.

He hadn't noticed the baseball lying where the terrified kids had dropped it and as he was backing away, he stepped on the ball. His feet flew out from under him and the gun flew from his hand. He fell flat on his back and as I saw the portly catcher in full gear fall on top of his exposed rib cage, I heard a sickening 'crack.' The boy's helmeted head snapped back catching the perp squarely in the mouth.

I charged forward, rolled the boy off the perp and the perp on his stomach and cuffed him.

As I stood, my toe caught the perp in his injured ribs and he let out a yelp of pain.

"OOPS!" Accident? Well, maybe not.

As the perp laid there, bent double, gasping for air, with a bloody mouth, it took some of the pain away from my own ribs and lip.

Lady Justice has an uncanny way of evening things out if you give her the chance.

If I had quit, these scumbags would still be out there ripping off the good citizens of Kansas City. However, I harbor no guilt about quitting football. Smartest decision I ever made.

CHAPTER 12

A WAVE OF PANIC had rippled through the real estate community. One of their own had been taken. Bulletins and alerts had circulated from the Board of Realtors to the offices and on to the agents. Take no chances. Meet no strangers. Go out in pairs. Stay alive!

And still, there would be yet another life this vicious killer would steal away.

We were met at squad meeting by a grim-faced Captain.

"Men," he said. "A second body has been found floating in Lake of the Woods in Swope Park. She has been tentatively identified as 24-year-old Samantha Greenwood, another real estate agent. Like Ms. Duncan, she was also nude and her body was covered with ligature marks. A similar note was found in a watertight bag taped to her torso. In the bag was a magazine ad with the caption, 'Rookie Of The Year.' Another note with letters cut from the same type of magazine read, 'Your Rookie of the Year is now my Nookie of the Year.' "

Sick bastard.

The Captain reviewed and compared the similarities of the two murders. It was plain and simple. We were looking for a serial killer who would probably strike again.

The victims were from different offices in different parts of town. One veteran agent and one rookie. They had never co-oped on a sale together. There was no obvious commonality other than the fact that both were women and both were realtors.

The officer from homicide who had been given the lead on the case was Detective Derek Blaylock. He's a 20-year veteran cop and considered to be the best in his division.

We spent the next hour reviewing the facts and evidence of the cases. Not much there. The autopsy had come back on Nancy Duncan. Death by strangulation prior to her being dumped in Loose Park Lake. Ligature marks, bruising and cuts and worst of all, evidence of severe trauma in her vagina indicated that Ms. Duncan had experienced an excruciating and painful death.

Forensics had found no physical evidence on the body or in the park around the lake.

The note was sealed in a Glad Bag that could be purchased in any supermarket and attached to her torso with duct tape available in any hardware store. The killer's note had used letters cut from the same realtor magazine as her full-page ad. You could pick up one of these at a hundred locations around town. Not much to go on.

Detective Blaylock reviewed the possible list of obvious suspects.

In a homicide, experience has shown that the first person to rule out is usually the spouse or significant other. Neither woman was currently married, and as far as co-workers knew, neither was involved in a serious relationship. Dead end there.

An obvious suspect would be a disgruntled client, but the Brokers of both agents knew of no trouble brewing. No complaints had been filed and, why, if a client were out for revenge on an agent for perceived negligence on their real estate transaction, would he attack a second agent with absolutely no connection to his deal? Keep looking.

Another possibility would be a jealous co-worker. As mentioned previously, real estate is a very competitive business, and is governed by the old 80/20 Rule. Twenty percent of the agents account for eighty percent of the business. There are a few really good agents and a whole lot of wannabes. But since agents in the course of their activities co-op with other agents, serve on committees together and socialize at Board functions, there is a VERY active grapevine. If you poop on another agent, the word spreads fast and your bad reputation soon spreads throughout the real estate community. So far, both women had spotless reputations. Aggressive? Yes! But fair and honest. Still with nearly two thousand members in the local Board, we couldn't rule out the possibility of another agent with a grudge. That's a lot of interviews and a lot of legwork.

With nothing else to go on at this point, the Detectives were concentrating their efforts interviewing family and co-workers trying to uncover the common thread that linked the two women to the killer.

After the squad meeting, I called Maggie. Of course she had heard the news and was devastated. I asked her if she knew the girl. She said she knew her by reputation only. Samantha had been an agent for just two years. She had been dubbed a rising star in the real estate community and, as the ad read, had earned the honor of 'Rookie of the Year.'

There's something about being young and successful that gives one a sense of invulnerability. Bad things always happen to someone else.

Not always.

Apparently, Samantha had been really pumped yesterday afternoon. She shared with her office partner that she had an ad call on one of her listings, a large 2-story home on Ward Parkway listed at $349,000. The house was vacant and ready for immediate occupancy and the caller said he could pay cash.

When you're young, eager and driven, caution often takes a back seat to ambition. Samantha never returned to the office.

Maggie shared that the real estate community was in a state of panic. Business had come to a virtual halt. No one was showing property unless the client was known and trusted.

"Maggie," I said, "I don't want you to set foot out of your office unless you call or text me where you are going and who you are with and when you will return. Do you understand? I don't care if you're just slipping out for a sandwich at lunch. I want to know. This guy is killing women just like you. You'd never know when you are being stalked and when he might strike again."

"I promise," she said, "I gotta go now." I heard her sob as she clicked the phone shut.

(HAPTER 13

EVEN THOUGH WE WERE ALL totally focused on the serial killer in our city, other criminals don't take a holiday from their nefarious deeds. In fact, the incidence of petty crime increases, as the bad guys know the police are preoccupied and spread thin over the city.

Ox and I were seldom assigned a specific case. We were usually on patrol or serving warrants. But with senior officers busy trying to apprehend our serial killer, we got a new assignment. The Senior Center Mugger.

The Thomas Swope Senior Activity Center is indeed the center of the universe for the growing population of golden agers. It is open every day of the week and the entire day is filled with a menu of activities designed to exercise the mind and body of the aging.

In one room octogenarians are decked out in spandex leotards and are learning to do a yoga exercise that would ward off arthritis.

Not a pretty sight!

There are card tables surrounded by women with naturally grey, bleached blonde, dyed black and brilliant blue hair, playing canasta or bridge.

In the corner, an old guy with boney knees wearing Bermuda shorts, sandals and calf length black socks may be playing pool with a grizzled ex-farmer in Big Smith overalls with a red bandana hanging out of his back pocket.

And you've got to understand the lingo. Getting a little action meant you didn't need your fiber that day. Getting lucky meant you found your car in the parking lot and an all-nighter meant you didn't have to get up and pee.

Something to look forward to.

A hot meal is served everyday. The cost is only $5.00 for those who can afford it. No one is turned away.

Friday night is bingo and Saturday night is a dance. Life is good!

Or at least it was until some enterprising thug decided that mugging seniors could be profitable.

Now you've got to understand we're not talking about Al Capone or Pretty Boy Floyd here. You take down a bank or armored car, you get thousands of dollars. You take down Mrs. Bergmeyer you may get $18.37. But you may also get her prescription drugs that can be sold on the street or occasionally a credit card.

And besides, it is making life miserable for the old folks. And life is too short.

Fortunately, no one had been seriously hurt. The guy's M.O. was to surprise the victim, sometimes on the way to the bathroom, which I have found is a frequent occurrence among the elderly, or on the way to their cars.

He's always dressed in a white sport coat with a pink carnation in the lapel and he wears a Richard Nixon mask. Now that's scary.

The Senior Center Administrator had tried to hire a Security Company to patrol the grounds, but operating on a tight budget, soon had to abandon the idea.

Midtown squad had been instructed to do as many drive-bys as possible, but with the Center open twelve hours Sunday through Thursday and fourteen hours Friday and Saturday, the chances of a black and white driving by at the moment of a mugging were slim.

Ox and I talked the situation over. We concluded that the presence of uniformed officers might, indeed, deter the mugger, but we wanted to catch him. He certainly wouldn't strike with us there. The solution we arrived at was to go undercover. YES!

I used to watch <u>The Streets of New York City</u> and <u>Hill Street Blues</u>, and I thought it would be so cool to work undercover.

Unfortunately you can't sell many houses as an undercover realtor. So, my dream had to wait.

Our problem was Ox. He's built like a tank and at 52 he's a good 25 years younger than the average senior population. Plus, he still has his own hair and teeth. That's a dead giveaway.

Our solution was, with the co-operation of the Center Administrator, to ostensibly hire Ox as a maintenance/janitorial worker. His job was to sweep floors, bus tables and clean the piss off the bathroom walls when the old guys miss. He was thrilled.

Now I fit right in. Sixty-five years old, a head of grey hair AND, I still have a powder blue leisure suit and a shirt with a Nehru collar from the 1960's in my closet. For some reason, I just can't part with them. I just know I'll attract the chicks like a magnet.

Thursday: Day one of the undercover operation at the Senior Center.

Ox is introduced at lunch to the assembled seniors. He busies himself bussing tables and emptying trash. The only event of any significance was when bussing a vacated table, Ox found a set of teeth the previous occupant had left by their plate.

Thank heavens for lost and found.

I, on the other hand, was doing my best to blend in. I had watched some of the guys playing pool. When they tired, I picked up a stick and looked around for a partner.

An old guy with a hump on his shoulder and a limp in his walk made his way to the table.

"Looking for a game, Sonny?" he asked.

"Sure," I replied, and we racked them up. Eight ball.

I'm no slouch at pool. My grandpa taught me to play when I was old enough to hold a cue and see over the edge of the table.

We seemed pretty evenly matched and finally only the eight ball was left on the table. We each missed a couple of shots and on his last shot he left me set up for a perfect kill shot. I slammed the ball in the pocket and he said, "Good game, Sonny. You want to make it interesting? Say--- uhh---$5.00 a game?"

Not wanting to be a piker or sore winner, I said, "Sure, $5.00. I won. You break."

He broke all right and then he ran the table. SUCKER PUNCH! I had been set up.

Just as he was pocketing my five spot, another old guy walked up. "New fish, Ernie?" and he grinned and walked away.

So much for Day 1.

Friday: Day 2 of the undercover operation at the Senior Center.
Nothing out of the ordinary.

Just old ladies in leotards with their asses stuck up in the air doing the 'Squatting Dog' or something like that. I tried not to look.

But, it's Friday and tonight is BINGO! Can't wait.

The games start at 7:00 sharp and run until 9:00. Cards are fifty cents each per game and the winner gets half the pot and the other half goes into a kitty for the grand prize on the last game of the evening.

Blackout.

The hall was packed. When I saw each player with a half dozen cards for each game, I did a mental calculation and figured that final pot would buy a lot of Metamucil.

Very methodically, the caller turned the drum filled with the precious little round balls. Each player was poised with their multi-colored dabbers, frantically searching and dabbing as each number was called.

The evening went smoothly and finally it was time for the big game. Numbers were called and everyone waited breathlessly as the cards began to fill.

Then: B-3

"Bingo!" shouted Mabel Whisler and she jumped to her feet and did a little victory dance. A collective moan was heard around the room. So near and yet, so far.

As the hall was clearing, Mabel was one of the last ones to leave. She was on the podium collecting her winnings. She stuffed the envelope in her purse and headed for the parking lot. But just as she passed a janitor's closet, the door opened and out stepped Richard Nixon.

"Time to pay your taxes, Mabel," he said, and grabbed her purse.

Ox was cleaning yellow stains off the wall beside the urinals when he heard Mabel scream. He bolted out of the can and stood face to face with Richard Nixon.

"You're about to be impeached," he snarled.

Seeing this mountain of muscle between himself and the door to the parking lot, Nixon did an about face and sprinted back past Mabel and into the Bingo hall.

I was just coming out the door when he blew past me. He was headed toward the emergency exit at the far end of the hall. As he leaped on to the podium, he gave the bingo table a flip. The cage with the balls flew into the air and crashed to the floor, exploding, and scattering bingo balls everywhere.

I turned to pursue, but I saw the disaster too late. My momentum carried me forward, I hit the sea of balls, my feet flew out from under me, and again, I saw those damn stars as my tailbone landed squarely on B-17.

I heard the emergency bell sound as the mugger burst through the exit and out into the night. What a disaster.

Our only consolation was that the mugger dropped Mabel's purse during his frantic escape.

Saturday: Day three of the undercover operation at the Senior Center.

There was excitement in the air today. Special occasion. The Seniors' Prom.

While the Center has a dance event every Saturday, this one is special. Just like high school, the hall is decorated with multi-colored streamers, paper tablecloths and centerpieces. The whole works. And, the coup-de-gras, A LIVE BAND!

The seniors pay $5.00 a pop to cover expenses. We figured that since the mugger didn't get away with his loot the night before, the take from the entrance fees might lure him to strike again.

After last night's debacle, we concluded that with so many people to watch in such a large area, we could use some extra eyes, so we invited Mary and the Professor to the Prom. At 75 and 85 years respectively, they, of course, would fit right in.

When I told the Professor of our botched job and of our plan for the evening, I was comforted by his words from the Master: "Our greatest glory is not in never failing, but rising every time we fall."

Great words to live by.

Mary, on the other hand, had a different spin on things. "Hell yes, I'll go," she said. "I love to dance."

As we arrived at the hall that evening, you could feel the electricity in the air.

Seniors love to dance. And I mean REALLY dance. Not just the stand in one spot and wiggle your butt with your hands in the air crap that youngsters today call dancing.

These people grew up in the Big Band era. Glenn Miller, Tommy Dorsey, Artie Shaw. Ahhhh! Those were the days. They knew how to waltz, foxtrot and swing. A few of the crowd even mustered up a tango.

There's something magical about seniors at a dance. You will see these good folks coming from the parking lot with walkers and canes and you immediately think, "Wow! This is gonna be a real hoot!" But the minute the music starts, it's as if 20 years and most of the ravages of their dotage have fallen away. They dance. And dance. And dance.

This evening was extra special because of the live music. Naturally, the band consisted of four old guys who billed themselves as: "The Grateful Not To Be Dead."

Where did they get that?

Our town is known for its' Kansas City Jazz. The 18th and Vine district is every bit as famous as Beal Street in Memphis or the French Quarter in New Orleans. There is even a jazz museum there. Good music has been coming from Vine Street since the turn of the century.

All the guys in the band had, at some time, played in the clubs or the fancy ballrooms of that era. You can take the man out of the music, but you can't take the music out of the man, and these guys would get together to jam at the drop of a hat.

We were all set. Ox busied himself in the hallway and bathroom area as he had on the previous night, to watch the main entrance. I had the Professor take a table by the little old gal taking the money and Mary was seated by the emergency exit. I circulated around the room trying to spot anything unusual.

The Professor was quite dapper in a brown tweed suit and bow tie.

And Mary had come in her best floral muumuu. I can only say that with this full billowing garment draped over her 200 pound frame, it looked like someone had pitched a rose colored tent over a Christmas tree. A sight to behold.

In fact, when Mary took her seat at the table, one old guy turned to his buddy and remarked, "Hey Ralph. Get a load of this. You gotta see it to believe it."

Mary fired right back, "Well Buster, then you better believe it, cause you ain't gonna get to see it." Can't get ahead of that girl.

Later that evening, an old geezer slipped into the chair next to her and whispered, "Hey, Sweetie, do you believe in the hereafter?"

"Well of course I do," Mary replied.

"Then you understand what I'm here after," he said.

Mary gave him a look that would peel paint and he quietly slipped back into the crowd to look for a more willing lass. If she were alive, Ruth Buzzi would be proud.

The evening was coming to an end. "Tuxedo Junction", "In the Mood" and all the old favorites had been played. Finally it was time for the last dance of the night. As the strains of Hoagy Carmichael's "Stardust" filled the room, every senior was on the floor. Wall to wall people.

Then suddenly, a figure burst into the room, grabbed the cash box and bolted for the door.

"There he is," someone shouted. "It's Nixon!"

As the night before, Ox emerged from the powder room to block the main entrance. I happened to be by the kitchen door on the opposite side of the room.

So the mugger, as he did last night, elbowed his way toward the emergency exit. Only tonight, standing between him and freedom was a 200-pound obstacle dressed in a pink floral muumuu with a 36" Hillrich & Bradsby.

He stopped short. Mary looked him in the eye, "You feel lucky tonight, Sucker, WELL, DO YOU?"

Dirty Mary.

The mugger's shoulders drooped, he dropped the cash box and with a sob, we heard Richard Nixon wail, "I am not a thief."

The lights came up as I approached the mugger. I cuffed him and as I removed the mask, a collective gasp came from the gathered crowd, "LOUIE."

"I didn't want to do it," he cried. "I didn't want to hurt anyone. Martha is so sick. She's dying of cancer. I needed the money ---- for her."

Stunned silence. One of their own had fallen.

We got our man.

Justice? I suppose so.

But sometimes I think Lady Justice wears that blindfold to wipe the tears from her eyes.

CHAPTER 14

WE HAD MISSED THREE DAYS of squad meetings while undercover and were anxious to find out what progress had been made in the apprehension of the 'Realtor Rapist,' as he had been dubbed by the press.

Bad news.

The autopsy on Samantha Green had produced exactly what was found on Nancy Duncan. Nothing. Same cause of death. Same trauma. Same torture.

Interviews with family and co-workers had produced no viable leads. Upon searching the victims' apartments, they found no evidence that indicated that anyone other than the occupant had been there. Dead-ends everywhere.

Then more bad news.

The Captain arrived looking weary and dejected. "Another body was found floating in Troost Lake," he said. "She's been tentatively identified as Lucy Lindquist, age 55, and, of course, a realtor."

The room fell silent. We were all doing our best, but it just wasn't good enough. A week had passed since the first murder and we were no closer to the killer than the day we started.

The bag taped to her body contained an article from a realtor periodical. The headline read, "Lucy Lindquist elected present of WCR, Women's Council of Realtors." The accompanying note read "Now she's the president of DBR, Dead Bitch Realtors."

According to Maggie, the realtor community had come together as never before. Each office had conducted classes on self-defense and how to use the pepper spray that each carried on their key chains.

Office policies had been put in place requiring agents to leave word with the office secretary of every scheduled appointment and agents were cautioned to go out in twos, if possible. E-mails had been sent warning agents to be wary of male cash buyers they didn't already know.

With everyone on high alert, the opportunities for the killer to strike at an open house or vacant house diminished.

So he took a different tack.

Apparently he had stalked Lucy and followed her home. Lucy lived in a high rise on the Country Club Plaza. The building had underground parking and the killer had followed her there and attacked as she exited her car.

Forensics had found traces of pepper spray and blood at the scene. Lucy had fought back. But she was no match.

The Captain introduced Dr. Cecil Billings, a forensic psychologist, a profiler.

His examination of evidence in the three killings indicated that we were dealing with someone whose violent rage was directed specifically toward powerful women.

Rapists, in general, fall into this category. Their hatred of women is manifest in their dominance and control of the women's minds and bodies and their ability to inflict pain. Some rapists are wound so tight they can't achieve penetration on their own, so they use other objects to achieve the end. This seemed to be the M.O. of this killer.

This hatred often originated early in life, initiated by a cruel, domineering or uncaring mother. Historically, these men cannot sustain a satisfactory long-term relationship and if they do marry, it ends in abuse and divorce.

These men are especially vulnerable to women in power. It's bad enough to have to endure these women in a social setting, but when subjected to a situation, such as at work, where a woman has been given a position of authority, the rage can boil over.

And trust me, these women are powerful. A top producing female agent didn't get there by being timid. Most have fought their way to the top and stay there by the sheer force of their will. You cross them, they will squash you like a bug.

After hearing Dr. Billings' report, the Detectives concluded that they should concentrate their efforts in the real estate community. The killer had the ability to lure his first two victims within the framework of normal real estate activity, indicating that he had some knowledge of how the system worked. And with Dr. Billings' characterization that the killer resented being subjected to powerful women, it was worth taking a closer look at intra-office relationships to see if they could uncover any antagonistic male-female struggle that, so far, had been under the radar.

CHAPTER 15

ONGOING CASES COULD NOT be ignored. Narcotics had been working on gang related drug distribution for months. Undercover officers had penetrated the inner circle of the 'Niners,' black gang-bangers operating in and controlling the area around the government housing projects on 9th Street.

A drug deal had been set up and Narcotics was ready to take down the boys in the hood.

All available officers were pressed into service. The area that needed surveillance was large, from Charlotte to Troost on the east and west and from Independence Avenue to 12th Street on the north and south. We were to dress in plain clothes so as not to attract attention, but to be available in the event any of the bangers slipped out of the net.

Ox and I were at Independence Avenue and Campbell. It's a mixed neighborhood with small retail stores on the corners and large, old, two story homes in between. This is an old part of town. Most of the homes were constructed at the turn of the century. Years of neglect had caused the neighborhood to deteriorate and several of the houses were 'board-ups,' houses that had been abandoned and doors and windows were covered with plywood to keep out vandals and druggies.

As the appointed time for the bust arrived, we waited anxiously for word that the party was over and all the bangers were accounted for.

But, instead, the message came over the walkie-talkie, "We have apprehended three subjects at the scene, but the leader of the Niners, Duane or 'Li'l D' as he is known, has escaped. He is a black male with dreadlocks, dressed in grey cargo pants, black shirt and black Nikes with a white check logo. Last seen he was heading north on Charlotte toward Independence Avenue."

Charlotte was just one block from our location and we headed in that direction. We spotted Li'l D sprinting across a parking lot heading for a board-up. We took off after him.

Just as we reached the board-up, we saw him disappear around the corner and down the old driveway beside the house. We were close behind but as we turned the corner, no Li'l D.

We surveyed the scene and Ox quietly put his finger to his lips and pointed to the base of the foundation.

In the old days, these big old homes were heated with coal. The coal truck would back into the driveway and shovel coal into a small opening in the foundation. A coal chute.

We looked at the hole, maybe eighteen inches square. We looked at Ox. NO WAY! We looked at me. OH CRAP!

It was dark town there. I could only imagine the insects, rats and other vermin that occupied this dark abyss.

"You got your stuff?" Ox asked. "Your gun, spray, cuff, flashlight?'

Flashlight?

Why would I bring a flashlight? It's the middle of the day.

"Let me take yours," I said.

"Don't got one neither," he replied.

Swell!

"You go in and see if you can locate the perp. I'll stay here by the chute and call for back-up," he said.

Sounded reasonable except for the 'me go in part.'

Then I thought, what would my heroes do? Sam Spade, Boston Blackie. No guts, no glory. So I lay on my stomach, stuck my feet in the hole, and inched myself backward until I could bend at the waist. I let my feet dangle hoping to touch something solid. Nope. Was it two feet or ten feet to the cellar floor?

"Well, in for a penny, in for a pound," I thought, and I gave a shove and launched into the darkness. I hit the floor, stumbled and crashed into some old paint cans stacked against the wall. If Li'l D didn't know we were after him before, he certainly did now.

I moved into the darkness and 'EEEUUUUW' my face was engulfed in a heavy sticky spider web.

You know how Indiana Jones hates snakes?

Well, I HATE SPIDERS!!

When I was six years old, Tarzan of the Apes was one of my heroes. I would go to the movies and see Lex Barker conquer the jungle bad guys.

In one movie titled <u>Tarzan and the Web of Arrack,</u> Tarzan was captured by a giant spider and woven into a silk cocoon. I've been scared shitless of spiders ever since.

I could only imagine the hairy beast whose home I had invaded and I let out a yelp as I brushed away the web.

No sooner had my lips opened when 'BLAM.' I heard a slug whiz past my head. 'Cripes,' nobody said he was armed and dangerous. Hmmm. Gang leader. Drug dealer. Fleeing felon. DUH!

I hit the ground and scooted across the floor for cover. I pulled my trusty revolver and tried to remember what Roy Rogers would have done when pinned down like this.

Li'l D must have heard me scoot and he fired off another round. This time I saw the muzzle flash. 'BLAM, BLAM, BLAM.' I fired three quick ones in Li'l D's direction.

I was somewhat on edge, this being my first gunfight. Suddenly there was a 'thud' to my right and I turned and fired again, 'BLAM, BLAM, BLAM.'

Then a voice came from my left side. LEFT SIDE? I had been suckered by the old 'throw a rock to confuse them' ploy.

Li'l D's voice came through loud and clear, "Well, copper," he said, "I counted six shots and I didn't hear you reload that peashooter. Now your ass is mine." And I saw his shadow coming for me in the dark.

"I shoot nine peas, not six," I replied, and fired a .22 long rifle at the approaching shadow.

I heard a scream as Li'l D hit the floor.

At that moment all hell broke loose. I heard a crash and wood splintering upstairs. A flashlight beam shone down the basement steps and illuminated the gloom. Hallelujah, the troops had arrived.

OR NOT.

The first thing I saw bounding down the steps was an 80-pound German Shepherd with jaws wide open. He clamped his enormous jaws firmly into my crotch and I felt the pressure as Mr. Winkie and the boys were held firmly in this toothy vice.

A light shone in my face and a booming voice shouted, "Don't move a muscle or you'll be singing soprano."

No shit!

"W-W-W-Walter Williams," I stammered. "I'm on your side!"

Ox had come in right behind the canine officer. "Oh crap," he cried, as he saw the big dog firmly gripping my privates. "That's my partner."

"Release," ordered the canine officer, and the Shepard backed away from my scrotum.

"Sweet Jesus," I muttered as I passed out and hit the ground.

I awoke to the irritating sensation of smelling salts. I was surrounded by officers and medics. Gingerly I felt between my legs. All the parts seemed to be there. What a relief.

"Li'l D?" I asked.

Apparently my blind shot had taken out his left nut. Not life threatening, but it would certainly bring a guy to his knees. It was probably a good thing he was going to prison. I didn't think he'd be starting a family anytime soon.

Irony is certainly not lost on Lady Justice. My manhood, such as it is, was spared. Li'l D's, not so much.

I'll take it. All of it. Well, maybe not the spiders.

CHAPTER 16

AFTER MY HARROWING EXPERIENCE with Li'l D and the Hound from Hell, I was exhausted.

Three days undercover and a drug bust hadn't left much time for my Sweetie. We had talked on the phone, but we needed an evening together. We decided we would go out for a nice dinner and see what developed from there.

My definition of a nice dinner and hers sometimes differ. My definition of fine dining is Mel's Diner on Broadway. I eat there a lot.

At Mel's you can get a platter of biscuits and gravy and two eggs any way you want them for four bucks.

When Mel fixes my favorite lunch, he plops a BIG glob of real butter on a piping hot grill and sautés sweet onions until are all gooey and sweet and don't taste like onions any more and he piles them high on a half pound ground beef patty with fries. All for six bucks.

In the evening, you can get a ten-ounce t-bone, a baked potato as big as a football and Texas toast for $9.95.

What a deal.

Mel has a sign over his cash register that says, "If you leave here hungry, you didn't clean your plate."

And gravy! WOW! For me, gravy is one of the major food groups. White cream gravy with ground sausage over biscuits, a hot beef sandwich with rich brown gravy and best of all creamy fried chicken gravy with the little pieces of the chicken coating floating around.

"Healthy?" you ask. Well, nobody's died at Mel's in 20 years so it can't be too bad. I once read that a person would be much healthier eating natural foods, so I tried. Then I read that most people die of natural causes, so I quit. I think I just missed Mel.

I picked Maggie up at her apartment and as we pulled away I asked if she had any preference in eating establishments, secretly hoping for Mel's. No such luck.

Maggie had heard of a new restaurant that had just opened in the old garment district downtown. That area had once been all factories, but as more and more labor was outsourced to our friends in China, the factories closed and sat empty for years. Then came the rebirth of downtown. Old factory buildings were converted to luxury apartments and condos and gobbled up by the yuppie elite.

Apparently, this new restaurant, Chez Francois, was opened to cater to the tastes of the new downtown gentry.

When we drove up, I knew we were in trouble right away. A large sign on the curb said "Valet Parking Only." I hate valet parking. I hate turning my keys over to a pimply faced kid with a stud in his lip. I hate waiting in line while they try to find where they hid my car. I hate tipping some jerk for something I'm perfectly capable of doing myself.

Thanks, I'm glad I got that off my chest.

We were escorted inside and as I looked around, my suspicions were confirmed. I'm in trouble. The building had once been one of the big, fancy hotels of the era. But with the decline of the district, it closed. The interior had been restored to its' former grandeur with high ceilings and ornate woodwork. Tables were set with fine linen cloths and sparkling crystal, and from somewhere the strings of a Bach fugue, or some such thing wafted through the dining area.

We were seated in a quiet little alcove and were soon approached by a waiter dressed in a starched white shirt and black tie and had on trousers with a pleat so sharp it would cut your finger.

His demeanor was somber and he walked like he had a broomstick up his butt.

He bowed and said, "Good evening, my name is Rolph and I'll be serving you this evening."

"Evening, Ralph," I replied.

"Excuse me, Sir," he said. "It's Rolph, not Ralph."

Oh shit, this can't be good.

"Uhh, yes, Roolph," I replied and muttered under my breath. "Whatever."

He laid a book the size of the Kansas City phone directory in front of me, "Our wine list, Sir," he said. "Would you like a moment?"

Well, yea!

I looked at page after page of wines but I couldn't find the Arbor Mist. "You do have Arbor Mist, don't you?"

Rolph looked aghast. "I don't believe we have that in our wine cellar, Sir." and stuck his nose in the air.

How can you have eight pages of wine and not have Arbor Mist? Go figure.

Maggie came to the rescue. "We'd like a bottle of your house chardonnay," she said.

"Very good, Ma'am," Rolph replied. He bowed and walked away.

I might as well share some of my other idiosyncrasies. I am neither poor nor uneducated. I didn't just fall off the turnip truck. But I am a simple guy. I come from a middle class, blue-collar background, but I have made a comfortable life for myself.

However, the affectations of the wealthy bore me and in my humble opinion are a real pain in the ass.

Maggie knows me well and I thought I saw a smile cross her face as Rolph and I did our verbal thrust and parry. She would have to be on her toes this evening.

Just then, a bus boy arrived with a woven basket of bread.

Hot dog.

Now we're getting somewhere.

He laid the basket on the table then produced two small platters and a jug that was filled with some viscous liquid that resembled 30-weight motor oil. He sprinkled some green stuff on the platters and proceeded to pour the Quaker State on top. "For your bread, Sir," he said and bowed.

I don't think so!

"You wouldn't happen to have a pat or two of butter back there, would you?" I asked.

"Very good, Sir," he replied, bowed again and headed off to the kitchen.

I opened the cloth cover of the breadbasket anticipating warm soft yeast rolls. Yikes! It might as well have been a basket of hockey pucks. In my mind, I could see Mel's Texas toast. Thick slices of soft bread lightly buttered and grilled to a golden brown and served piping hot to your table.

Dream on.

Have you ever tried opening one of those things? A hammer and chisel should come with them as standard equipment. And, if you do manage to penetrate the outer shell, crumbs are everywhere. I tried and, sure enough, crumbs were everywhere. No sooner had my roll exploded in my lap, Rolph approached with a tiny silver dustpan and a tiny whiskbroom.

"Excuse me, Sir," he said, and proceeded to whisk away my crumbs.

Just think of all the labor they would save by serving soft bread.

I wonder if they have a suggestion box?

Soon Rolph returned with our bottle of wine, a bucket of ice and two glasses. He set one glass in front of me and with the skill of a surgeon he whipped out his corkscrew and popped out the cork. Gotta hand it to old Rolph. It came out in one piece and he didn't even need the Black & Decker.

He poured about one swallow in my glass and stepped back. I thought, "Well hell, I paid forty five dollars for that bottle. I ought to get more than that. And even worse, he didn't even give Maggie any."

I looked at Maggie. She grinned at me, nodded her head toward the glass and said, "How about you give it a taste and make sure it's right for us."

Oh right! Maggie saved my sorry ass again. I tasted and Rolph waited for my response. "It's Ok," I replied. "But it's sure no Arbor Mist."

Rolph turned and walked away.

He returned with menus.

"What's good tonight, Roolph?" I asked. Just friendly banter with the waiter. Right?

He stiffened, "Sir, everything from our kitchen is good."

OK then. It was really just a rhetorical question.

We studied the menu. When I say studied, I'm serious. You'd have to be fluent in three languages to read the damn thing. "Do you know what any of this stuff is?" I asked Maggie.

She shrugged her shoulders and frankly I was relieved when she said, "Not really." I hated being the only dummy.

Rolph returned with order pad in hand and looked expectantly in our direction.

Maggie spoke first. "I'd like a shrimp cocktail and your house salad with creamy Italian dressing, please." Maggie had been watching the calories, so I didn't know if her order was weight watching or a cop-out on the menu selections.

Now understand, I've got nothing against salad. I even eat it sometimes. But man didn't get to the top of the food chain by grazing. We're carnivores, after all. I needed meat.

I pointed to the menu and said to Rolph, "Maybe you can help me out here. Where's the beef?"

I thought I detected a slight flinch, but Rolph replied without hesitation, "May I recommend, Sir, our beef tenderloin medallions, garlic whipped potatoes and vegetable medley."

"Sounds good to me," I replied. Meat, potatoes and vegetables. Can't be too bad.

Our dinners arrived. A huge bowl of salad and a glass with shrimp butts sticking out the top was placed in front of Maggie.

I looked at my plate. Yikes! There were two tiny pieces of meat, each about the size of a fifty-cent piece and each was covered with a teaspoon-sized dollop of mashed potatoes. On the left side of the plate were two carrot spears and on the right, two asparagus spears. Yellow gunky stuff was dribbled around the edge of the plate and a sprig of something that resembled the weeds I spray in my yard was sticking out of the mashed potatoes.

"Lovely presentation, isn't it, Sir?" Rolph gushed.

"Presentation my ass!" I thought. "Where's my dinner?"

But to Rolph I replied, "Lovely, just lovely. You wouldn't happen to have some gravy back there, would you?'

Wounded, he replied, "We don't serve GRAVY here, Sir," and he walked away.

It didn't take long to finish dinner.

Rolph returned with another menu. "Would you care to order dessert, Sir?" he inquired.

I was still hungry and I was thinking of Mel's pies. Lemon, chocolate, coconut cream. Six inches high with creamy filling and fluffy white meringue. "Sure," I said and took the menu.

OK, they had flambé, brule and a torte. Where's the pie?

Rolph returned. "Your order, Sir?"

"Two tortes," I replied, "and two cups of coffee." And off he went.

He returned with a dainty little cup about the size of a big thimble. My heart sank as I thought of the giant mugs of steaming coffee at Mel's. You could sit and drink all day for $1.95. I was paying $6.00 a gulp.

I turned to Rolph, "Do you give refills?" I asked. Without even a nod he turned and walked away. I think I was getting on his nerves.

He returned with our tortes. Do you know what a torte is? Well, I didn't either, but I soon discovered it was a little square piece of pastry not much larger than a postage stamp. It doesn't even have icing. But, all kinds of colored syrup were dribbled around the plate in a fancy design. Humph, Picasso torte. But what good was it. The only way it could be eaten was to lick it off the plate and after what I'd seen so far, I didn't think that was an option.

Oh, yeh. Presentation. Bullshit!

By the time I had paid my bill, tipped Rolph and the valet, I had dropped a couple of c-notes. I could have eaten at Mel's for two weeks for that kind of money.

Probably won't be back.

We had avoided talking about the 'Realtor Rapist' at dinner. Just getting through the meal was stressful enough.

On the way back to her apartment I related my latest adventures in crime fighting. She was shocked to learn that I had actually been shot at and horrified that she had almost lost Mr. Winkie to the Hound of the Baskervilles.

She invited me in for a cup of hot chocolate and a cookie. Maybe two cookies. I was starving.

We finally got around to the elephant in the room. The murders.

I told her about Dr. Billings' profile of the murderer and that the detectives were now concentrating their efforts looking for someone within the real estate industry, either an agent or an affiliate, who might have an axe to grind with women of authority.

It was hard to get her head around the idea that someone so close to home could commit such atrocities. It would be so much easier to believe that the killer was a total stranger.

I had been an active agent for 30 years, but had been retired about six months by this time. Maggie, of course, was still entirely immersed in the business. Between the two of us, we knew most of the agents in most of the offices.

I asked her what had been in the grapevine just before the murders started. There was always scuttlebutt circulating about whom was screwing whom, both figuratively and professionally. Nothing startling. There were a few dalliances of note and agents were always grumbling about how some competitor had stolen their client, but certainly nothing to evoke the violent rage exhibited by the killer.

Earlier in the evening I had formulated a plan to turn Mr. Winkie into Mr. Happy, but by this time we were both so exhausted I discovered he had become Mr. Sleepy. Not wanting him exposed as Mr. Dopey, I kissed her goodnight and said goodbye.

I cautioned Maggie again not to set foot out of her office without a call, e-mail or text letting me know where she was going, who she was going with, and when she would return. She promised.

CHAPTER 17

THE NEXT MORNING I went out to retrieve my newspaper and discovered that Willie had retrieved it first. He was sitting on the front step absorbed in the headline:

"POLICE ARREST SUSPECT IN THE 'REALTOR RAPIST' MURDERS"

I didn't realize I had been out of the loop. The bust must have taken place the night before when I was sharing the evening with Maggie and Rolph.

"Shit, man," Willie exclaimed, "I jes don believe dis is happenin'. Dis jus ain't right."

"What's not right, Willie?" I asked.

"Dis here," he replied and pointed to the story under the headline. "Here you read it."

The headline read that the police had finally found a common link between the three murdered women. All three drove luxury cars and all three had their car regularly cleaned and detailed by Leo's Luxury Car Service.

Leo Snipes had recently been estranged from his wife of 15 years and was apprehended sleeping on a cot in the backroom of his service bay by Officer Lincoln Murdock. Although Snipes declared his innocence he was not forthcoming with an alibi for the nights of the murders. Snipes is being held in the city jail pending his arraignment.

"What's the problem with this?" I asked. "The guy fits the profile. He has a connection to all the victims and he certainly has an axe to grind with women, just being kicked out of his home."

"I'll tell you what's wrong wif dis," he exclaimed. "I been knowing Leo for ten yeas o' mo. An I KNOW Leo ain't no killer. Sure, he used to boost some stuff like me, but he ain't never hurt nobody. And he been straight, like me, since he opened his shop."

"An dat deal about being 'estranged,' shit, man, Leo and Doris been fightin' as long as I been knowin' 'em. Doris always knew Leo was fooling around, but couldn't never catch him."

"Leo always liked the women. Hell, I 'member one time he was kiddin' around and he say, 'Willie, a girl's panties may not be de bes thing on earth, but dey next to it.' "

"I bet Doris finally caught Leo doin' de nasty with ole Charlene and kicked his black ass out o de house."

"That may all be true, but if he's truly innocent, he surely must have an alibi for at least one of the nights of the murders." I said.

"Yea, he probably got an alibi, all right. He jes don wanna say it. Charlene's old man drive a truck over de road. I bet he outta town and Leo be over der boinking Charlene and he don wanna say nuffin to protect her. And hissef too. Charlene's old man is one mean dude."

"Do you think Leo would talk to me?" I asked.

"Probably not, lessn maybe I give you a note tellin' him you OK. Dat might work," he replied.

So, I got a note from Willie and went to the City lock-up. Normally, I wouldn't stand a chance of getting to talk to a suspect, but since our recent collars, Ox and I had achieved a celebrity status. You know, The Dynamic Duo, and all.

I was admitted to a holding cell and Leo was brought in wearing cuffs and shackles. I explained who I was and read Willie's note. He still was reluctant to talk to me, so I decided to just go for it and I told him I knew about Charlene and why he was reluctant to use her for an alibi.

"Shit, man," he said. "I can't be draggin' Charlene into dis. Her ole man beat de crap out o' her if he find out."

"Just tell me the truth," I said. "If you were really with Charlene, that means the real killer is still out there and will kill again. Do you want that on your conscience?"

"O' course not," he said. "Yea, I was wif Charlene. Wot am I gonna do?"

"Tell you what," I said. "I'll keep this to myself for now. Captain Short is a personal friend of mine. I trust him. Let me talk to the Captain and see if we can substantiate your alibi without having to expose Charlene publicly. OK?"

I went directly to Captain Short's office and told him everything that Willie and Leo had told me. While he had hoped this arrest would bring an end to the nightmare, he understood that if the wrong man was locked up, the killer would certainly be free to claim another victim. He said he would personally go to Charlene and, if she could substantiate his story, he would get it on tape.

I like this guy.

I was feeling pretty good about myself. I was in the locker room getting my gear ready for the day when someone grabbed me from behind and slammed me into the wall. Murdock.

Apparently the word had traveled fast that I had spoken to Leo.

Murdock had me pinned up against the locker with his forearm across my throat and his knee in my crotch. He got right in my face and shouted. "What the fuck you doing talking to my collar, old man? You got no business talking to prisoners. You aren't even a cop. You're a damn civilian playing cop. I'm warning you for the last time. Keep your hairy old nose out of my business." And he shook me, let me go, and I dropped in a heap.

"Well, that could have gone better," I thought.

I was enraged that he was so shortsighted that he would rather preserve his collar than put the right man behind bars.

But I was even more upset by his remark. What did he mean 'hairy old nose?'

I am meticulous about my grooming. Maggie makes sure of that.

Now I do understand the problem. I have found that as I grow older, my hair follicles are migrating south. As the years have passed I have discovered I have less hair on my head, but overall, I haven't really lost it. It just relocated to my ears, nose and eyebrows. And Maggie doesn't like it.

It's a constant battle keeping ahead of the little guys. Have you ever tried clipping the hairs out of your ears? First of all, how do you see in your ears? It can't be done. I tried once and almost gave myself a lobe-botomy. Since then, I have to slip my barber, Mac, a couple of extra bucks to trim the forest out of my ears. And boy, do these babies grow fast. Sometimes, I think someone is pouring Miracle-Gro in my ears when I'm asleep.

And don't get me started on the nose hairs. Where do they come from? Back when I was selling, Maggie said to me, "How can you expect your buyers to concentrate on your contract when all they can think about is that big grey thing sticking out of your nose?"

Real Estate 101.

And even worse, I've picked Maggie up for an evening out and as we're driving along I noticed Maggie looking at me. I'm expecting, "Oh, sweetie, I really missed you today," or "I've really been looking forward to this evening." Instead, I get "You might want to tuck that thing back up in your nose 'til you get home tonight."

Great. That always sets the mood for a romantic evening.

I hate clipping nose hairs. But a man's got to do what a man's got to do, so I bought a Remington Turbo. It scares the shit out of me when I think about sticking Turbo up my nose. I'm always afraid it will pull instead of cut. You ever pull out a nose hair? Hurts like hell. And it sounds like a Black and Decker, which doesn't help. But, it does have a little light that shines up my nostril before I plunge.

High tech.

Maggie doesn't like bushy eyebrows either. She says I look like Wilford Brimley. You know, the old guy who does commercials on TV and looks like he's got two white hairy caterpillars chasing each other across his forehead. Don't want that, so I have a tiny little pair of scissors that Maggie got me for Christmas sitting on the shelf by my Remington Turbo.

The gift that keeps on giving.

The next morning I opened my newspaper and was relieved to see the headline: "SUSPECT RELEASED IN 'REALTOR RAPIST' MURDERS. POLICE BAFFLED."

The article went on to say that police had substantiated an alibi for Snipes on the nights of the murders. No names were mentioned. "Whew."

Lady Justice had prevailed. Murdock would be really pissed.

I ran into the Professor. Naturally, he was curious as to the progress of the case. I shared with him all that I knew up to this point, including the psychologist's profile.

I could see the wheels turning in that old grey head, trying to mesh the information we currently had, with his years and years of experience.

Finally, he spoke: "Man who fart in church, sit in own pew."

"Excuse me," I said. "What in the world are you talking about?"

"Let me put it in the popular vernacular," he said. "In other words, never crap where you eat!"

"Oh, that really clears it up." I said.

"Listen Walt," he said. "You need to be looking for a guy who up until now has worked with these powerful women, but was able to keep his rage in check. Then something happened that upset his delicate equilibrium and caused him to go over the edge. He initiated some event that caused a shift in his relationship with women, possible putting him in a subservient position."

"I see where you're going, Professor, I said. "I'll give this some thought and see where it leads."

I drove to the station thinking about what the Professor had said. It sure made sense, but where do you start? With a hundred different offices, large and small, and several thousand agents, the possibilities of interaction are endless. Add to this the fact that the three victims were not in the same office and had no ongoing disputes, there didn't seem to be a common thread that would cause these women to be specific targets. Only that they were successful women with honorary titles and position of authority. Hmmm!

Maybe these women had absolutely no connection to the killer. Maybe they were simply surrogates and symbols of the powerful woman that had caused the killer to act. We knew the killer was no dummy. So far, he had left no clues and no witnesses.

Think about it.

If you're pissed at someone close to you and you kill them, who do the cops look at first? That's why the spouse is always the first person questioned. Eliminate the people closest to the victim. So, if you're smart, you will pick a victim removed from your frame of reference. That's why random killings are the hardest to solve. No obvious connection.

The professor's words rang in my head. "Never crap where you eat." The killer was purposefully targeting powerful women outside his circle of influence. He was hiding in the anonymity of two thousand agents while the police were looking for a connection where there was none.

After squad meeting, I asked the Captain if I could have a moment of his time. What could he say? After all, Ox and I had three good collars in a week.

I shared with him my thoughts on the case and told him I'd like to take some time to personally visit some offices and chat with some of my old realtor buddies. Having been in the business, I might possibly pick up on something that an outsider would miss. "Can't hurt," he said. "Do you need Ox?"

ROBERT THORNHILL

"Probably not," I said. "He'd just scare everyone to death."

So with the Captain's blessing I started making the rounds. I began with the offices and agents I knew well. By the end of the day, I was so wired with caffeine I could hardly sit still. Everyone wanted to chat over a cup of joe.

No luck. Everyone was concerned and no one had a clue. So I went home.

CHAPTER 18

UPON ARRIVING AT MY APARTMENT building, I noted that Willie was busy with a large plastic trash bag tidying up the front lawn.

As I approached, I heard him mutter, "God sho mus love stupid people cause he made so damn many of 'em."

"What's up, Willie?" I asked. "Why so grouchy?"

"I just don understand how folks can be so filthy. I been clen' up people's shit all day long. Mary called this monin'. Told me Billy Jenkins had moved out of #8, so I went over der to clean de place up. Whole damn room full o' trash. Dat boy been dere six months and I don't tink he been to de dumpster even once. Pizza boxes, beer cans, you name it, dat boy lef' it. Dis-gustin."

"An' den, I gets home and dere's shit all over dis here front lawn. I jus' gets so pissed off that people so damn stupid."

"Well you know what the Professor always says," I replied, trying to inject a bit of good humor: "It's better to be pissed off than pissed on." Willie didn't find that humorous.

"Yea, well," he muttered, "when I'se do one whats got to clean it up, I gets pissed on and off bof."

Just then Bernice Crenshaw emerged from the building. Bernice is 83 and was an elementary schoolteacher until she retired. Bernice lives in 2-B across the hall from the Professor. She has been with me about ten years and the Professor and I have noted that Father Time has been taking his toll. Her short-term memory seems to be slipping and we're afraid Alzheimer's may be creeping up on her.

For those of us in our golden years, Alzheimer's is even more scary than cancer or a heart attack. The thought of slowly losing our ability to think, remember the things we accomplished and recognize the ones we love is frightening.

Sometimes we make light of the things we fear the most. It's our way of coping. We trivialize in order to take away the power of that which we fear. Alzheimer's jokes abound and that's OK unless they're cruel.

I remember the Professor addressing the subject one day, "There's more money being spent on breast implants and Viagra today than on Alzheimer's research. By 2030, there will be a large elderly population with perky boobs and huge erections and absolutely no recollection of what to do with them."

There! Take that, Alzheimer's.

Bernice shuffled up to us, "Oh, I'm so glad you're here! I'm afraid I've locked myself out of my apartment again. I was going out to get my mail and as I was going out the door, I couldn't remember if I had turned off the stove, so I went back in and checked the stove. Sure enough, I had left it on, and I laid my keys on the counter and turned off the stove, but then I couldn't remember what I was doing before I went back into the kitchen, so I decided to sit down and write a letter to my sister. That made me remember that I was getting the mail and I got so excited that I remembered, I ran out the door without my keys."

Oh boy!

"Not a problem," I said. "Willie can get you back in. By the way, Bernice, how have you been feeling lately?"

"Well, to tell the truth," she replied, "I've been feeling kind of lonely. I've been thinking I might go visit my daughter in Topeka for a few days. But I can't stay there very long. It's my son-in-law. He's a real ass. He reminds me a lot of my husband."

I hadn't heard her speak of her husband before, and assuming he had passed way, I asked, "I'm so sorry about your husband. When did you lose him?"

"Didn't lose him," she replied. "Kicked his sorry ass out then divorced him --- for religious reasons."

"Religious reasons?" I queried.

"Yes," she replied. "He thought he was God and I didn't. Always bossing me around. Telling me what I could and couldn't do, where I could and couldn't go. So, I just finally told him where he could go."

Whoa, this was a new side of Bernice we hadn't seen before.

"It really does get lonely living alone," she said. "I miss Bitsy, my little Peekapoo."

"What de hell's a Peekapoo?" Willie asked.

I explained that it was a dog. A Pekinese that had been bred with a poodle was a Peekapoo.

Willie pondered that for a moment. Then with a gleam in his eye he whispered in my ear, "If dat's true, den if you breed a Bulldog with a Shiatsu, does you get a Bullshit?"

Everyone's a comedian.

After our misspent evening at Chez Francois, Maggie and I decided to try it again. We planned to grab a bite to eat and take in a movie.

Since she got to pick the restaurant last time, it was now my choice. You guessed it. Mel's. Maggie was thrilled.

I had a chicken fried steak and mashed potatoes smothered in white cream gravy. Ummmmm! It doesn't get much better that this. I can't remember what Maggie had, but whatever it was I'm sure it didn't fit in her diet. We were, after all, at Mel's.

I was enjoying a mug of steaming coffee with a piece of chocolate cream pie when a sharp pain in my back hit me like a bolt of lightening. My arm involuntarily jerked and I slopped steaming coffee into my lap. That'll get your attention. I couldn't decide which hurt worse, by back or my dick.

"What in the world is wrong with you?" Maggie cried. She's used to my idiosyncrasies, but this was outside the box, even for me.

"Wow! Don't know," I replied. "It felt like someone just hit me in the back with a rubber hose. It's easing up now. I'll be OK." And I started drying myself with a napkin. Good thing I had on dark trousers. At my age, someone might mistake my little accident with incontinence.

As we sat in the movie, the pain in my back intensified and spread around my left side. It would subside and then return with a flourish. Every time it struck again, I would squirm. I finally was squirming so much I was distracting everyone around us. Dirty looks. I couldn't concentrate on the movie plot and by the time it was over, I had no idea what we had just seen. It really didn't matter. It was a chick flick and I probably wouldn't have understood it anyway.

Earlier in the day, Mr. Winky and I had discussed the possibility of him becoming Mr. Happy tonight, but as we drove home Mr. Back had the final word and the message to Mr. Winky was, "No way!"

I dropped Maggie at her door, returned home, and spent most of the night pacing the floor in pain. In the morning I dressed and went straight to Doc Johnson's office.

After spending what seemed an eternity in the waiting room, the nurse called me back, took my temperature and blood pressure and had me stand on the scale. She took the reading and gave me a glance. "It's the chicken fried steak," I muttered.

She asked what had brought me into the office and I told her of my night's ordeal.

"Here," she said, "go pee in this cup and wait in room #3. The Doc will be right with you."

First of all, I don't like doctors. Not Doc Johnson. He's OK. Just doctors and hospitals in general and all those places that smell funny. And I especially don't like peeing in a cup. I don't really know why. When I was a kid, my buddies and I would write our names in the snow and see who could pee the highest and farthest. But somehow that's different than peeing in a cup.

Anyway, I finished and waited in room #3. Pretty soon Doc Johnson came in. "Got blood in your urine, Walt," he said. "You might be passing a kidney stone. I'm going to send you across the street for a CT scan. Let's see if we can find the little bugger."

Swell!

I'd heard about these things and nothing I'd heard had been good. In fact, I didn't know anyone who had said, "Gee, I wish I had a kidney stone!"

So, I went to the radiology lab and was escorted into a little room. The nurse said to strip and put on this little gown hanging on the door and someone would come get me. Who invented these gowns, anyway? Why don't they go on like a robe, with the slit in front? And why is there only one tie and it's in the back? You put the damn thing on and then you have to walk around with your hand clutched behind your back so your ass won't hang out.

Then Nurse Ratchett walked in. Why do all my nurses have to look like her? My hiney did a little pucker as I remembered my last encounter with her counterpart.

She led me to a room with a sliding table that I was to lie down on. The table would then slowly carry me forward into this giant tube with whirling lights. "This won't hurt a bit," she said.

"Yea," I thought, "it won't be hurting you!"

As the table slowly moved me toward that gaping hole all I could think of was James Bond in <u>Goldfinger</u>. He was strapped in a similar machine that was moving him and his privates toward a burning laser.

Remember that one?

I closed my eyes and gripped the side of the table. The machine whirred and pulled me out. It was over and I still had my privates. What a relief.

I returned to Doc Johnson's office and again waited in #3. The Doc came in and said, "Yep, Walt, you're about to give birth to a 4mm kidney stone."

Lucky me.

"So what do I do?" I asked.

"Just drink a lot and pee a lot," he said. "It will naturally come out by itself. I'm going to give you a prescription for an antibiotic. We don't want you getting an infection. And also a pain killer, if you need it."

Great. Painkiller. Just what I wanted to hear.

So I took the prescription to Wally Crumpet, the pharmacist at Watkins Drug store.

I handed Wally the prescription and said, "What's he giving me, Wally?" I can never read what a doctor writes. They must have a special class at pharmacy school to learn to read doc-write.

"Well, it looks like Sepra and Naproxen," he said.

"What is it and what does it do?" I asked.

"Well, the Sepra is an antibiotic and Naproxen is Aleve, a pain killer," he said.

"Why didn't he just say Aleve?" I wondered.

"Most drugs have two names," he said. "Tylenol is Acetaminophen, Advil is Ibuprofen and Aleve is Naproxen,"

Right.

He thought for a moment and with a sly smile said, "I bet you don't know the other name for Viagra?" I shook my head.

"Mycoxafloppin."

Pharmacist humor.

"Oh," he said, "You'll be needing this too." And he whipped out a tea strainer. "Use this to catch the stone. The doctor will want it to have it analyzed."

Great. Now pee in a strainer. That's worse than a cup.

I paid for my prescriptions and returned home.

Willie was sitting on the porch. "Hey, Mr. Walt," he said. "I heard from Leo. He said tell you if ever need yo car shine, jes come on by. It's on the house. Where you been all day?"

I told him about my physical impairment.

"Ohhhh, Mr. Walt," he said, "I knowed a guy had dem stones. Like to damn near killed him. He moaned and groaned for days. Had to pump hisself full of dat Valium stuff to keep from screamin'. When he finally passed 'em, it was like shootin BB's out his pecker."

Willie, you're such a comfort.

I spent the rest of the afternoon and early evening drinking and peeing through a strainer. I need a hobby. I had just started a stream when I got the feeling that someone had put a blowtorch to Mr. Winkie.

Then, 'Plop,' there it was. Right there in the strainer. I had given birth to a tiny little piece of gravel. My very own kidney stone. It looked like it might be a girl, so I name it Pebbles. You know, like Fred and Wilma's kid.

CHAPTER 19

I HAD LOST A DAY with my labor pains but I had spent the entire day before, visiting realtor friends and offices and had come up empty.

Even with my background, I was faring no better than the detectives. The thought of another day spent shooting the bull with old cronies seemed pointless.

We were missing something. Out there somewhere was an interpersonal struggle that had enraged the killer and sent him over the edge. What was it that was so stressful as to cause this grievance?

GRIEVANCE!

Why hadn't I thought of this before?

Relationships within the real estate industry are very complicated and governed by law. There are the relationships between clients and realtors, between realtors from different companies, between realtors in the same company, between realtors and their offices, etc., etc. Most of the time everyone gets along and if there is a dispute of some kind, folks will usually sit down and come to a rational compromise.

Not always.

Those cases that cannot be resolved amicably are submitted in writing to The Grievance Committee of the Board of Realtors. This group of real estate practitioners reviews the complaints that are submitted and if they believe they have merit they are sent on to the Professional Standards Committee for a formal hearing. Cases with no merit are dismissed.

Why try to find the needle in the haystack? Why not look in the pincushion?

I drove to the corporate offices of the Board of Realtors and asked to see Stella, the Executive Secretary of the Board. She had been there for years and knew everything that was worth knowing in the real estate world.

Naturally, she was devastated at the carnage within her industry and surprised to learn that I had traded my briefcase for a pair of handcuffs. The detectives in the case had interviewed her as well as the other Board officers, trying to discover the link between our killer and the victims. They, of course, found none.

I explained my line of reasoning and asked her if there were any cases currently assigned to The Professional Standards Committee. She said that there were currently six cases scheduled for formal hearing, but they were, of course, confidential.

"Stella," I said, "how long have you known me?"

"That's not the point, Walt," she replied. "Those files are sealed until after the hearing and final determination."

"OK, then, how about Nancy and Samantha and Lucy? And how about the next one of our colleagues that is found floating in a lake? Please, Stella," I begged. "Just let me take a look at the complaints. I'm not in the business anymore. I don't give a rat's ass who's arguing with whom. I just want to nail this guy before he kills again."

She sat motionless for several minutes. I could sense the internal struggle. She had to decide if the breach in protocol could be tolerated for the greater good. An ethical woman with a moral dilemma. I had always admired and respected her.

She retrieved the files and locked me in a conference room.

"Knock on the door when you're finished," she said.

And I went to work.

There were six cases pending. Not many surprises as I looked through each one.

It was the usual run of the mill stuff. A claim from a buyer that the agent didn't disclose knowledge of a leaky basement, an agent complaining that another agent had approached her seller for their listing while it was still listed with her, yada, yada, yada. Serious stuff to the participants, but petty in the overall scheme of things. Certainly nothing to inspire mayhem.

Then, there it was:

Case #1343
Complainant: Julie Bowen
Respondent: Jack Ballard
Charge: Sexual Harassment

BINGO!

I hurriedly read the file and made notes. Jack Ballard was the Broker-in-Charge of Upjohn and Associates, Realty. Julie Bowen, an agent in the office had filed a complaint stating that Ballard had, for some time, made suggestive remarks and sexual innuendos toward her. She had tried to ignore him but the situation came to a head when he called her into his office under the ruse of a broker performance review and he made physical advances toward her.

The case had been reviewed by The Grievance Committee and sent on to The Professional Standards Committee for a hearing.

I knocked on the door and Stella entered.

"Stella," I said excitedly, "what do you know about this Jack Ballard case?"

"It's so sad," she said. "Jack was never a real popular broker, but he ran a tight ship and kept the agents on their toes and you know how difficult it is to find a good broker, so the owners overlooked his personality flaws to keep his organizational skills. But things changed after Julie filed her complaint. The owner knew that if the complaint was justified and they did nothing they could find themselves being sued for negligence. So they relieved Jack of his broker duties until after the hearing."

"Don't tell me," I said. "Let me guess. He was replaced by a woman."

"That's right," Stella replied. "Brenda Martin was installed as broker at Upjohn."

As I drove back to the precinct, the Professor's admonition jumped into my mind: "Man who fart in church, sit in own pew."

Ballard had farted in his church and was up to his perverted neck in pew!

This had to be it. I couldn't wait to get back to the precinct to report my discovery to the Captain.

CHAPTER 20

AS I WAS PULLING INTO the precinct parking lot, my cell phone vibrated. I looked and the screen said, 'One new voice mail.'

"Oh crap," I thought. I had turned off my phone while in the Board Office and had missed a call.

I dialed up voice mail and heard Maggie's sweet voice, "Hi, Honey, just doing what I promised. We got loan approval on Campbell today so I set up a termite inspection on Cherry Street. It's about 10:30 now. I'm meeting Ajax Exterminating at 11:00. Maybe we can grab a bite of lunch afterward. Give me a call and let me know if you are available. Otherwise, I'll make other plans. Bye. Love you." And she hung up.

I checked my watch. 11:20. Still plenty of time to catch her for lunch. I could visit with Captain Short after lunch and I rang her cell phone. No answer. Straight to voice mail.

Hmmmm! That's not like Maggie. She always picks up. She's always afraid that next caller might be a cash buyer. On the job 24/7. That's the life of a realtor. So I dialed again. No answer. Straight to voice mail.

A chill suddenly racked my body. Surely not Maggie! Just my imagination. After all she's not meeting a stranger, it's Ajax for heaven's sake. But I couldn't shake the feeling.

I called the real estate office and asked for Joan, the office secretary. Protocol now dictated that agents had to leave detailed accounts of their coming and going with the secretary.

When Joan came on the line, I said, "Hey Joan. It's Walt. Maggie left a message she was going to a termite inspection on Cherry Street. Do you have the exact address? And while you're at it, could you look up the phone number for Upjohn Realty in the Board directory?" "And, oh," I added, "could you see if Jack Ballard's address is in the directory, too?"

"Sure," she replied, and soon came back on the line with the information.

I was about ten minutes from the Cherry Street address so I headed that direction hoping to catch her there with the inspector.

I felt a wave of relief as I pulled up behind the panel truck, which read, "Ajax Exterminating. If it crawls, it falls. If it flies, it dies."

Clever.

Maggie's car was parked just ahead of the panel truck, so I had caught them both.

I hurried to the door and rang the bell. No answer. "Must be in the basement," I thought, and rang again. No one came. So I knocked. No one came.

"Gotta be around back checking the foundation, so I circled the house."

Nobody there.

My feeling of relief was replaced by panic.

I rushed around the house and back out to the panel truck. The sliding side door was closed but not locked. I slid the door opened, and to my horror, discoved the blood soaked body of the termite inspector.

"My God! Maggie!"

After all we had done, after all our precautions, he had found a way to claim another victim.

Only this time it was personal.

It had to be someone with intimate knowledge of an agents' activities and scheduling. Someone who would know when your guard would be down and you'd be vulnerable.

JACK BALLARD!

I called 911 and reported the location of the body. I didn't want to identify myself and be tied up the rest of the afternoon with red tape. I had to find Maggie!

I knew in my heart it was Ballard. It all fit. But just to be sure, I dialed the Upjohn Realty office and asked for Ballard. I'd feel pretty stupid making accusations when he'd been in the office all morning. But he wasn't. No one had seen him today.

I knew I didn't have much time. The bodies of the other victims had been found the morning after their abductions. I had no way of knowing if he killed them quickly or waited until the cover of darkness. My guess, judging from the condition of the bodies, was that he took his sweet time and inflicted as much pain as possible before he killed them. My stomach lurched as I thought of Maggie in the hands of this human garbage.

I had Ballard's address. It was on Rockhill Road near the UMKC college campus, about fifteen minutes from my location.

I called Ox on his cell. "Hey, whatcha doing, partner?" he bellowed as he saw my number flash on the screen. "I've been missing you."

"Ox, I need your help," I said. "He's got Maggie." I explained what had transpired and asked him to meet me at Ballard's home.

We didn't want him to see us and provoke him to expedite his twisted plan, so we agreed to meet on the next block and approach on foot.

Ox arrived about five minutes after I did. By this time it was 12:30. By my calculations, Maggie had been with him about an hour and a half. We had to hurry.

Like most of midtown Kansas City, this was an old, but well maintained neighborhood. Large two story homes sat on spacious lots and mature trees and shrubbery shaded the lawns.

Ballard's home faced Rockhill Road but backed up to the rear of a house on the street behind it. We approached from that direction. Using the bushes and trees for cover, we made our way to the back of his house. A double car detached garage sat at the end of the driveway. I motioned for Ox to check out the garage. In the meantime, I worked my way around the corner to get a view of the street. No cars at the curb or in the driveway. I returned and Ox shook his head.

Nothing in the garage.

Quietly, we worked our way around the house, peering into both ground floor and basement windows. No light on. No signs of life.

"If he's got her here, it has to be on the second floor," I said. "We've got to get in."

"We can't go in without a warrant," Ox replied. "Anything we find won't hold up in court."

"I don't give a damn about rules of evidence," I cried. "Maggie could die while we're waiting for a piece of paper. I'm going in!"

As quietly as possible, I broke a pane of glass in the back door and reached in to turn the lock. We entered cautiously with weapons drawn and searched the first floor and basement.

Clean.

We crept up the stairway and peered down the dark hallway. Three bedrooms and a bath. One by one we checked them out. Nothing.

SHIT!

Maggie wasn't here. With the mutilation we had discovered on the bodies, I had expected to find at least traces of blood or evidence of a struggle. The bodies were nude. Maybe Ballard had kept articles of their clothing as trophies. But there was nothing to indicate that any of the victims had ever been in the house.

Maybe I was wrong. Maybe Ballard wasn't the killer. Everything had seemed so right, but there was nothing here.

Then I saw it. By the telephone. Just a small business card, but on it were the words, "Ajax Exterminating. If it crawls, it falls. If it flies, it dies."

YES!

I know I'm right. But where are they?

Then a thought crossed my mind. This is Ballard's home of record. He was smart enough not to kill Julie Bowen or Brenda Martin. It was too close to home. He would have been an immediate suspect given his recent troubles, so he got his revenge on powerful women with whom he had no connection.

Same here.

He was smart enough to know that should he ever become a suspect, the police would find no evidence here. The Professor had it figured all along. Ballard was smart enough to know not to crap where he ate.

But where then?

"Maybe he owns another property," I thought. I went into his office and booted up his desktop computer. There is a program realtors and other professionals use called Jackson County Information Service. It is used to cross reference property ownership. You can enter an address and search for the owner of record of that property or conversely, you can enter an individual's name and all property owned by that person would come up.

I entered Ballard's name and up popped two addresses, the Rockhill Road address and an address on Duncan Road in Blue Springs.

Blue Springs is a bedroom community suburb of Kansas City. This was out of my service area when I sold and I had no idea where it was. I pulled up Mapquest, typed in both the Rockhill and Duncan road addresses and hit 'Get Directions.' Immediately a map with printed street-by-street directions came up. I hit the print button and we were on our way.

As we sped east through town toward Blue Springs, I studied the map. Blue Springs has grown by leaps and bounds over the last twenty years, but there is still rural property, small farms, on it's outskirts. Duncan Road was in a rural area.

It was now 1:30. Two and a half hours with the killer, but he had driving time too. Fortunately the I-70 freeway runs from downtown Kansas City straight east to Blue Springs. We had taken Ox's black and white so that we could use lights and sirens to bull our way through busy freeway traffic.

We talked about calling for backup, but what would we say? We had no evidence, no hard proof of any kind that Ballard was the guy.

I didn't think, "Hi, Captain, it's Walt and I've got a hunch----" would get much attention. We were on our own.

We followed Mapquest and exited I-70 and went north on Woods Chapel Road to connect with Duncan. The farther we went, the fewer houses we saw. We watched rural mailboxes for numbers and knew we were getting close.

Open fields were green with tasseled corn or soybeans. Some fields had just been hayed and massive round bales weighing several hundred pounds sat in the fields like giant monoliths. When I was a kid, I baled hay with my grandfather, but the bales back then were small and square and weighed maybe 40 pounds each. I helped him 'buck' the bales on the wagon and take them to the barn. The front of the second story of the old barns had an opening for the hay to be hoisted to the 'haymow,' at it was called. A track ran along the beam of the barn and a sliding pulley with ropes was used to lift and move the hay around the barn. Today, massive tractors with four-foot solid steel bale spikes spear the bales and load them on flatbeds. That's progress.

As we grew near, Ox killed the lights and siren. We pulled up to a mailbox and read the numbers. This was it.

It was a working farm. It had probably been Ballard's old family homestead. I knew he couldn't have been an office broker and a farmer too. Just not enough time in a day, so I figured he probably leased the land out to neighboring farmers who tilled the ground for shares of the crop. They worked the land, but didn't live there.

Perfect spot to commit murder.

We surveyed the lay of the land. A long driveway led to the old farmhouse. To the east of the house was a machine shed and the old hay barn, typical of the era, with open stalls below and storage for hay above. Implements of all kinds were parked around and in the barn. Mowers, round hay baler, hay rake, and of course the big green John Deere tractor with it's massive spike pointed skyward had the place of honor in front of the barn.

And there was a car in the driveway.

The farmhouse had deteriorated and it was obvious that it had not been occupied for a very long time. The boards in the porch floor were rotted or missing, pieces of rusted gutter hung from the eaves and bricks from the chimney were scattered about the ground.

We approached the side of the house keeping low to the ground. We slowly rose and peered into what we determined was the kitchen window. The house was built in the old 'shotgun style.' The front door opened into a living room, which opened into a dining room, which opened into the kitchen, which had a back door leading to another covered porch.

We could see Maggie. She was tied to a hardback chair. On a table by her side was an array of knives, clamps, pliers, and other hardware obviously collected by Ballard to inflict pain and death.

We didn't see Ballard immediately, but as we watched, he soon appeared. In his hand was a metal object about an inch and a half in diameter and eight inches long. It was an old window weight used years ago as a counterbalance inside the window framework that allowed the window to slide up and remain in place.

I remembered how the three victims had been assaulted and torn and I shuddered.

"We've got to do something fast," I whispered to Ox. "You take the front and I'll take the back. Let's count to twenty-five. That will give each of us time to get in position. On twenty-five we bust in, back and front. He won't know what hit him."

Ox pulled his Glock and I pulled my revolver and we moved to our respective positions.

Twenty-two, twenty-three, twenty-four, TWENTY-FIVE.

I hit the back door with my foot and the rotted casing gave way. Ox hit the front at the same time.

"POLICE, FREEZE!" Ox barked.

Ballard stood frozen. He saw we were both armed and he dropped the window weight and raised his hands.

Maggie sobbed.

I rushed to Maggie's side, laid my gun on the floor and began to cut the ropes that bound her with a knife from the table.

Just as I got her free, Ox came forward to put the cuffs on Ballard. He got halfway across the room and we heard a 'crunnnnch.' The old rotten floor gave way under Ox's 220 pounds and he disappeared in the basement.

Ox was gone, my gun was on the floor and Ballard saw his opportunity. He ran out the back kitchen door and disappeared around the corner of the house.

Maggie didn't seem to be injured, just frightened. "Stay here and check on Ox," I said. "I'm going after Ballard."

As I rounded the corner of the house, I saw Ballard disappear into the barn. I followed and peered around the corner into the barn. A dozen places to hide. Stalls, grain bins, equipment. He could be anywhere.

Then 'BLAM!' I heard the unmistakable sound of a 12-gauge shotgun. Pain shot up my arm like I had been stung by a thousand bees and my pistol dropped away. I must have only taken a few of the buckshot because I knew a well placed shot from a 12-gauge could almost cut a man in two. I dropped and rolled for cover as I heard the second round explode into the wood above my head.

Then I heard the 'click' as the shotgun was broken open. Ahh, a double barrel. He's reloading. And as I scampered to my feet I saw the wooden ladder leading to the haymow above. "He'll have a hard time climbing that ladder with a 12 gauge," I thought. "Maybe I can buy some time."

I climbed the ladder as fast as my injured arm would allow. It hurt like hell, but apparently nothing was broken and I could use it sparingly.

I climbed into the mow and saw that it was maybe half full of the old square bales of hay. They had probably been there for years. The upper hay door was open allowing light to enter. The hay was stacked against the back wall and rose almost to the ceiling. I saw the rope hanging down from the old hay pulley and I grabbed it and used it to pull myself up to the top of the hay near the ceiling. I remembered reading somewhere that in a fight, the one with the higher elevation had the advantage.

Just as I scrambled to the top, 'BLAM!' Ballard had followed me up the ladder. Pigeons scattered and splinters flew as the buckshot barely missed. I quickly figured that the higher elevation didn't seem to be much of an advantage when your opponent had a 12-guage.

I had just ducked behind a bale when 'BLAM!' I felt the bale shudder under the impact.

Then 'click.' He had popped the gun open for another reload. I peeked over the bale and saw him standing in front of the haymow door.

Just as Luke Skywalker, in moments such as this, summons strength from his Jedi Masters, a thought came into my head.

I looked at the old pulley overhead hanging from the I-beam that ran across the roof to the open door and the rope dangling from the pulley a mere two feet from my hand, and I remembered how many times I had seen MY hero, Tarzan, grab the vine, swing through the air, and vanquish his foe.

I looked again and my rational self said, "There are a million things that could go wrong." But then I heard 'click' again.

"What the hell," I thought. "Let's do it." "AAAAEEEEAAAEEEHHHHHHAAAHHH!" I screamed as I grabbed the rope and launched myself in Ballard's direction.

A look of sheer surprise and unbelief flashed across Ballard's face as my feet struck him squarely in the chest. The gun flew from his hand and he disappeared out of the haymow door.

I dropped to the floor and peered out the door. There below was Ballard, impaled on the massive hay spike of the John Deere.

It was over.

Maggie and Ox arrived just as I came out the door.

We stood for a moment looking at the bastard that had taken the lives of four good people and had nearly taken the life of the person most precious to me.

The three of us embraced. And we wept.

Justice had prevailed.

But at what price?

CHAPTER 21

AFTER OUR CLOSE BRUSH with death, we were spent. Our bodies were racked with pain. My arm was bruised and swollen where the buckshot had been removed and Maggie's feet and wrists were raw where she had been bound. We needed a break to recuperate and recharge.

We both had learned that our old bodies don't heal up as quickly as they did twenty years ago. One day you wake up and realize your skin is paper-thin and bruises like a ripe peach. But even worse, skin that once, when pinched, would bounce back like an elastic band, now just hangs there like a blob.

We needed to get away and clear our minds of murder, mayhem and Jack Ballard.

We decided on a trip to Branson, Missouri. Branson is about a four-hour drive south of Kansas City. It has been dubbed 'The Entertainment Capitol of the Midwest.' It is nestled in the hills of the beautiful Missouri Ozarks and is surrounded by crystal clear lakes and streams.

Branson has flourished over the past twenty years. Everybody who used to be somebody has built a theatre and has a show. Resorts and golf courses have sprung up like weeds.

We couldn't wait to get away from the city.

We threw our suitcases in the car and took off. The city traffic soon became the suburbs. Asphalt and concrete gave way to lawns and subdivisions.

We drove on and the 'burbs' became small towns.

About five miles past Osceola, Mo., we saw a large billboard which read "Gordon's Orchard."* Another sign told us that fresh peaches were available.

I love all kinds of fruit. I have apples, strawberries, grapefruit, honeydew, cantelope and papaya in my fridge when they are in season.

I also have bananas, but as Chiquita Banana says, "You never put bananas in the icebox."

Maggie saw the sign first. "Ohhh, can we please stop?" she begged.

She didn't have to beg very hard. I was already turning up the drive.

We pulled up in front of the large open market and we saw crates of cantelope, racks of tomatoes, boxes of blackberries as big as your thumb and bushels of perfect ripe peaches.

We roamed through the market, our mouths watering as we looked at the jams, jellies, honey and, of course, the fruit.

We were puzzling over the different varieties of peaches available when a wiry little senior with a salt and pepper beard and a leather 'Indian Jones' hat approached us.

"Can I help you with anything?" he asked.

"What's the difference in all these peaches?" I replied.

I soon discovered that you don't want to ask one of these country guys a question if you don't have time to listen to the answer.

In the next fifteen minutes, we learned from our new friend, Bob Gordon, everything a city boy would ever want to know about peaches. We learned that Bob and his wife Kay had been in the orchard business almost thirty-five years. You didn't have to listen long to know that Bob knew what he was talking about.

As I listened to him talk, I recalled a bit of wisdom I had heard from the Professor: "Choose a job you love, and you'll never have to work a day in your life."

I think that fit Bob perfectly.

We bought a basket of peaches and some red, ripe tomatoes. As I was checking out, I saw a basket of black, nut-looking things on the counter for twenty-five cents each.

"What are these?" I asked the cashier.

"Those are buckeyes," she replied. "You carry them in your pocket for good luck."

Considering what Maggie and I had just been through, I figured we needed all the luck we could get. So, I bought one for each of us.

We passed signs directing us to Bear Creek, Tin Town and Diggins. They sounded like fun places, but they would have to wait until another day.

We passed by fields of hay, corn and soybeans, which finally gave way to the rolling hills of the Missouri Ozark Mountains.

We stopped at the Branson Tourism Center and picked up our show tickets and a map of the Branson area. I looked at the map and saw red, green, blue and yellow routes and the famous 76 Country Boulevard surrounding and bisecting the city. I was curious as to the purpose of the colored routes and soon discovered their job was to keep you off the bumper-to-bumper traffic of the 76 Strip.

Guess where we were?

As we crawled along the Strip at a snail's pace, I began looking at our fellow tourists. Old people everywhere! I thought I'd died and gone to Florida. Old people were in cars and busses and standing in lines at restaurants and shows. And no wonder. There are roughly 130 shows going on in Branson at any given time and they definitely cater to the tastes and more importantly, to the memories of the elderly. Shows range from Andy Williams to Dick Clark and from John Wayne to Roy Rogers. Occasionally we would pass a water park or miniature golf course and see kids, but this was definitely a golden age utopia.

76 Boulevard. Miles and miles of tourist traps. Restaurants, theatres, miniature golf courses, motels and shops selling authentic Ozark Crap.

I saw a theatre playing, <u>Noah's Ark, The Musical,</u> and a Titanic Museum. A thought crossed my mind. The Arc was built by amateurs and the Titanic was built by professionals. Hmmmm!

Even the non-tourist businesses had a tourist oriented twist. We passed a radiator shop and the sign read, "The best place in town to take a leak."

The sign on a medical building read "Gynecology. Dr. Jones at your cervix." How would you like that guy staring at your twat? I had always wondered why your OB/GYN leaves the room when you're undressing and putting on that silly gown when he's gonna be looking up there anyway?

After an hour of breathing elderly exhaust fumes, we emerged on the far end of the Boulevard and followed the map to our resort, The Chateau on the Lake. Wow! What a place. Built in the style of a magnificent castle you might find in Germany or Austria, it perched on a high hill overlooking beautiful Table Rock Lake. Just the place to take your mind off a near death experience.

Or so I thought.

We checked into our luxurious room overlooking the lake and we saw ski boats, cruisers and jet skis streaking across the crystal blue waters.

"Oh, Walt," Maggie gushed, "doesn't that look like fun?"

I had other fun on my mind but Maggie really wanted to ride a jet ski, so we donned our bathing suits, jumped into the car and drove to the Marina.

We rented two jet skis for an hour, and I have to admit, I was exhilarated as we sped across the water, rooster tails sprouting in our wake. I glanced at the speedometer and realized we were clipping along at thirty-five miles and hour.

Suddenly, a huge cruiser that looked as big as the Titanic from my perspective, passed us going in the opposite direction. I saw it coming, but I couldn't avoid it, a three-foot wave generated by the gigantic cruiser.

Geronimo! I hit the wave at an angle, the ski became airborne and flew four feet in the air. My heiny rose up off the seat and my feet flew back just enough to let gravity take over so that Mr. Winkie and the boys hung suspended in mid air. Not for long.

The jet-ski hit the water with a 'SMACK,' my butt hit the seat with a 'SMACK,' and guess what was in between?

I moaned, doubled over and thought I was going to pass out right there in Table Rock Lake. Needless to say, we didn't spend our full rental hour on the skis. We drove back at a snail's pace, every little wave exacerbating the pain in my swelling gonads.

Our room had a lovely balcony facing west and looking out over the lake. We sat, side by side on the balcony watching a beautiful sunset while I clutched a bag of ice to my privates. Mr. Winkie was definitely on the blinky.

After the ice melted, we dressed and went for a nice dinner before our show. We had chosen a country show for the evening, you know, singing, dancing, fiddle playing, and goofy guys telling goofy jokes.

We arrived at the theatre and as I pulled into the parking lot I thought I'd arrived at the Greyhound Bus Terminal by mistake. There must have been twenty busses lined up side-by-side coughing out their noxious fumes. The Senior Tour Busses.

As we watched the busses spewing forth their human cargo, I did a little mental math. Hmmm. Twenty busses each holding at least fifty seniors, multiplied by 130 shows -----. A scary thought crossed my mind. If some politician was concerned over the national debt, a well-placed bomb in Branson and the resultant drop in Social Security and Medicare payments would go a long way toward wiping out the deficit.

We got our tickets and proceeded to our seats. I couldn't believe our good fortune. Seats one and two, second aisle from the stage. I figured that since our trip was a last minute thing, we'd probably be sitting in the nosebleed section.

As I sat there contemplating our good fortune, I heard the tromp, tromp of a hundred feet. I turned in my seat and thought I was watching a reenactment of the Bataan Death March. A robust woman carrying a red flag high over head was leading fifty seniors, who followed dutifully behind. The leader stopped directly in front of me and then I realized, Heaven Help Us, we were seated right in the middle of the Grey Hair Seniors Tour from Great Bend, Indiana.

The front row filled up and the lady with the flag gave me a look that said, "Move it over, Buster." So I swung my legs into the aisle so the seniors could fill the rest of our row. All was going well until a portly gentleman passing directly in front of me broke wind. If I hadn't clipped my nose hairs with my Turbo before we left, they would have surely curled.

At that moment, I remembered a word of wisdom the Professor had once shared with me: "A crowded elevator always smells different to a midget." I gained new respect for the challenges of the little people.

We really enjoyed the show. Finally, as it was drawing to a close, the emcee introduced a segment of the show that paid tribute to the men and women who had served in our armed forces. They had prepared a medley of the anthems of the various branches of the service and they asked the veterans in the audience to stand when they heard the song of their branch of the service.

As "Anchors Aweigh" played, I looked around and saw maybe a dozen men and women come to their feet. Some grey haired, some bent and wrinkled, some in their sixties, some in their seventies, some in their eighties, but all who had served their country proudly in Vietnam, Korea or World War II.

Then came the anthems for the Army, the Coast Guard and the Air Force and with each song a new group stood proudly representing their branch. Lastly, the words, "From the Halls of Montezuma to the Shores of Tripoli---" and the Marines proudly took the floor.

As each group stood, I noticed that many of them proudly wore caps with their units emblazoned in gold. These were the men and women who, in their day and time, had served Lady Justice and Lady Liberty so that succeeding generations could continue to be free. These were the men and women who represented those who had paid the ultimate price for our freedom. These were our real heroes. I thought of all those who had gone before and had given their service. And then I thought of the rest of us who still had service to give.

I had come looking for something to recharge my batteries and I had just found it.

The entire cast came to the stage and as they sang the stirring verses of Lee Greenwood's "God Bless The USA" the audience stood as one and I knew Lady Justice was in good hands.

Having recharged the spirit, it was now time to recharge the body before we returned home.

The resort has a wonderful Spa in which your body can be pampered in every way legally possible. On rare occasions, Maggie would indulge herself in a spa day at the Country Club Plaza, but I have to admit my shadow has never darkened the doors of a Spa.

Maggie oohed and aaahed as she read the services that were available.

For a price, of course.

The spa menu might as well have been in a foreign language because it was all Greek to me, so I relied on my sweetie and told her whatever she wanted to indulge us in it would be fine with me.

Big mistake.

Everything started off OK. We were led to an infinity whirlpool bath where we immersed our bodies in the fragrant churning waters. Then we were taken to the massage room where strong fingers erased the tension in our bodies. Then things started going downhill. Just as I was really getting into this massage thing, some gal showed up and started putting scalding hot rocks on my back.

'Yeow,' I passed on that part.

"Well, where next?" I wondered as I was led into another room. I was somewhat dubious when I saw the sign that said, 'Salt Scrub' but then under it were the words, 'Whole body exfoliation to renew, stimulate and moisturize.' That didn't sound too bad.

Wrong! Do you know what exfoliate means? I didn't then, but I sure do now. It means they're going to take off the top layer of your skin! With SALT, no less. Hasn't anyone ever heard of the old saying 'pouring salt in an open wound?' That's another way of saying 'IT HURTS!!!'

And exfoliating?? After I thought about it, isn't that what the Air Force did to the jungles of Vietnam with Agent Orange and napalm?

After I'd finished with that portion of the inquisition, Maggie said, "There's just one more thing I'd like you to do. I know how much you hate grooming and trimming, so they've got a treatment here that will eliminate at least one of your grooming tasks."

"Cool," I thought. "One less thing to trim is OK by me."

So they took me into a room and had me sit in a chair under a sign that said, 'Eyebrow shaping.'

So I sat.

A sweet little gal came in, laid me back in the chair and put a towel around my neck. She put this little patchy thing between my eyebrows and poured some sweet smelling goo on it and said, "We'll just let this set for a minute."

OK.

In about 10 minutes she returned. "Well, Sir," she said. "Are you ready?"

"Ready for what?"

RIIIIIP! "AHHHHHHH!"

No wonder Wilfred Brimley looks the way he does. I don't blame him.

Our last evening in Branson. We had decided to see Andy Williams. All the way into Branson we had seen billboard after billboard advertising his show. And there, bigger than life on those billboards was Andy, just like I remembered him from his TV shows with Donny and Marie. We were really looking forward to it.

We took our seats among the other golden agers and anxiously awaited his entrance. Finally, after a rousing fanfare, out into the stage stepped ----- 'YIKES!' An Andy Williams' zombie!

Who was this guy? He was old, grey haired, stooped and wrinkled. Then it dawned on me. This guy's eighty-two years old. What did I expect him to look like?

I sat there waiting to be disappointed and then he opened his mouth and the sweet, full, melodious strains of "Moon River" filled the auditorium. The room exploded in a huge round of applause and then fell silent as Andy crooned the verses of that famous song.

I looked around the room at the grey heads and I saw wrinkled old hands reach out and take the hand of the loved one next to them, and I saw tears glisten in old eyes as they relived their youth.

I reached over and took Maggie by the hand and I think maybe a tear rolled down my cheek, too.

Probably just allergies.

Later that evening, Maggie and I took a cruise of our own down Moon River. Captain Winkie piloted the ship into a safe warm harbor and weighed anchor for the night.

We were up bright and early the next morning, ready to head back to Kansas City.

We were several miles out of Branson when we spotted a sign along the road that said, "Fresh Farm Laid Eggs. Next Left"

"Ohh," Maggie wailed, "let's get some fresh eggs. I'll make you the best omelet you've ever tasted when we get home."

How can you turn down an offer like that?

So we made the next left turn and cruised into the driveway with a 'Fresh Eggs, Please Honk' sign. I honked and we got out of the car.

As I closed the car door, I saw two enormous golden retrievers bounding our way. The first one to arrive came right up to me and stuck her snoot in my crotch and sniffed.

What is it with big dogs and my crotch?

At least this one didn't have her jaws open.

The front door opened and a farmer in Big Smith's stepped out. "Get down Lady," he barked.

"That's certainly no lady," I thought. "A lady wouldn't sniff your crotch on a first date."

Then her companion approached and I assumed he was a male when he hoisted his leg and squirted on my shoe.

Farm life.

"Wot kin I do for yer foks?" he asked.

"We'd like a dozen eggs," I replied. "And a towel to," I thought, but I didn't ask.

As I looked around, I saw chickens of all sizes, shapes and colors roaming about the yard.

Funny looking creatures.

A thought occurred to me that everything in this old world has to begin somewhere. Who do you suppose was the first guy that pointed to a chicken and said, "See that chicken over there? I'm gonna eat the next thing that pops out of it's ass."

Think about it.

The farmer returned with the eggs and said, "That'll be a dollar and a half."

What a deal. A dozen eggs, a crotch sniff and a shoe shine all for a buck fifty!

Contented, revitalized and rejuvenated, with eggs in hand we headed toward home.

CHAPTER 22

ON MONDAY MORNING after our exciting weekend in Branson, I was summoned into Captain Short's office.

"Have a seat, Walt," he said. "I have something I want to discuss with you. This past weekend, there was an executive committee meeting attended by the Mayor, the Police Commissioner, the Chief, and the Commanding Officers of the various divisions."

"Wow! Must have been an important topic," I said.

"Walt, the topic was you," he replied.

OH Crap! "Just let me ex ---"

"Don't say anything. Just listen," he said. "While your methods have been somewhat unorthodox and in some cases not quite in accordance with standard police procedure, you and Ox have compiled quite an arrest record. In a relatively short period of time you've collared two muggers, a drug dealer, and the worst serial killer the city has seen in fifty years. And you're not even an officer -----yet."

"Yet?" I thought. "What the heck does that mean?" But I kept my mouth shut.

"Sometimes," he continued, "bureaucracy has a way of instituting hard and fast rules and over time the purpose and validity of those rules is lost, but they continue to be perpetuated because, 'that's just the way we've always done it'. Sometimes we have to take a step back and re-examine our priorities."

"I'm sure there was a time and a place where admittance rules regarding height, weight and age were valid. But we live in a different day. We came to realize that your collars were not made in spite of your age, but because of your age and past experience. You were able to bring something to the table that none of our regular officers possessed. You have helped open our eyes to new possibilities."

"Having reviewed our options, the Executive Committee has drafted a resolution that will be presented at the next City Council meeting which will eliminate age and physical requirements for officer candidacy. Division Commanders will be able to accept or reject candidates based on background and experience."

"Should this resolution pass, and I think it will, The Executive Committee would like to offer you a position on the force."

Dumbfounded, I sat there like an imbecile with a silly grin on my face.

"I'll take that as a yes," he said, smiling.

"And there's more," he said. "You can't be the only senior out there who thinks he's Hopalong Cassidy. There must be others who will want to come forward when the news is made public. What we need is someone who has been there and done that, who can help these old guys AND gals become oriented into the system. After orientation they will partner with a younger officer like you have been with Ox. We would like you to be that someone.

Plans are underway to create a new squad, the City Retiree Action Patrol. What do you say?"

What could I say but "YES!"

I was so elated. I hurried to the locker room to get my gear and came face to face with Murdock.

He and a dozen other officers were at their lockers preparing for their shift. Murdock grabbed me by the collar and squeezed. "Think you're pretty hot stuff, don't you old man," he snarled. "You may be hot shit now, but you're gonna get what's coming to ya. Mark my words."

"Let him go, Murdock." We both looked and a dozen officers had gathered around us. Dooley, a young officer spoke up, "A man's actions speak louder than his words. And guess what, Murdock? This old gentleman's been speaking a hell of a lot louder than you lately. How about you lay off and we'll all just go about our business OR we can do it another way."

Murdock looked around the room for support. Finding none he let me go and stalked out of the room. One by one the officers shook my hand. "Nice collar," they said. And I remembered something the Professor told me once: "Virtue is not left to stand alone. He who practices it will have neighbors."

Lady Justice and I live in a great neighborhood.

The day flew by and everyone I shared the news with was delighted.

Ox gave me a big hug and said, "I'm mighty proud of you, partner."

Mary said, "Great, maybe you can crack the whip on some of these scumbags around here."

The Professor said: "It is better to light one candle than to curse the darkness."

Willie said, "Shit man, a real cop. I accidentally get my ass throwed in jail, you get me out, right?"

Not even.

Maggie rolled her eyes and smiling coyly said. "Ohhh, my hero!" Now that's got some real possibilities.

The resolution passed the City Council and a date was set for my induction and the initiation of the City Retiree Action Patrol.

On the day of my induction, I sat on the podium listening to the politicians pontificate, I looked out into the audience. There, right in front of me, were all the people I cared about. I looked at the smiles lighting their faces and my heart was filled with joy.

As a boy, I was awed by my heroes, and like Superman, I dreamed a boy's dream of fighting the good battle for truth and justice. That dream, while dormant, never died, and here I was, sixty years later, and that dream had become a reality.

My name is Walter Williams and that's how I became a cop.

P.S. Only after all the articles were published in the newspapers and all the forms and brochures had been printed did someone discover to their horror that the acronym for the City Retiree Action Patrol is CRAP! And it's my baby!

(HAPTER 23

NOW THAT ALL THE HOOPLAS and attaboys were over with, it was time to get down to business.

Administrative guidelines and a step-by-step induction procedure had to be developed and submitted to the Executive Committee for approval.

In real estate, the volume of paperwork is so staggering that every time we sold a house, we killed a tree. By the time everything had been submitted for the City Retiree Action Patrol, we had wiped out a forest.

In the end, the procedure was fairly simple. Captain Short was put in charge of the group since I had originated under his command and since he so whole-heartedly supported the program.

It was my responsibility to review any applications that were submitted and if they passed my muster, the Captain reviewed them again.

Any applicants that passed both reviews were then subjected to the same three qualifying procedures that I had to pass, a written exam, a physical and the Oral Review Board.

Application requirements were fairly simple. The applicant must be retired from other full time employment, have no criminal record other than traffic violations, and no drug or alcohol abuse.

A press release announced the initiation of the program and the public relations office received a flood of inquiries from bored and lonely seniors looking for something to spice up their lives.

Once they discovered that the program involved more than just being a street crossing guard or Officer Friendly, the majority backed away.

Of the few who made it past the Captain and I, only one survived the three tests.

His name is Vince Spaulding. Vince is sixty-five years old and just retired from his forty-year position as a high school coach.

He was drafted by the old Kansas City Athletics right out of Junior College. He was an outfielder and apparently had an arm like a cannon. He rose quickly from Triple A to Double A, and had been invited to spring training with Kansas City. Then it happened. He blew out his knee sliding into home plate and that, for all intents and purposes, ended his professional career.

He finished college and over the next forty years, coached baseball, track, swimming and wrestling at several different schools. His most recent position, which he had held for fifteen years, ended when the Board of Education decided it was time for some younger blood, and put him out to pasture.

Vince was perfect for our program. He had no work related ties. He had been married for thirty-five years, but his wife died of cancer two years before his retirement. He was a man with social skills having dealt with Boards, teachers and parents for so long. He was healthy and fit and, most importantly, he just wasn't ready to sit down and quit. He felt like he still had something left to give and after lengthy conversations, we both agreed that C.R.A.P. was right for him.

He sailed through both the written exams and the physical. I had coached him on my ordeal with the Oral Review Board. But even that went smoothly. Vince is a trim 175 pounds, all muscle, no fat. While I came across to Captain Harrington and others on the Board as Casper Milquetoast, it was apparent that Vince could handle himself. No challenges from Harrington. He probably figured, and rightly so, that Vince could kick his ass.

Having been a wrestling coach, he was able to get through PT without kicking the instructor in the nuts, and after several practice days on the range, he qualified with the .45 Glock.

His first day at the precinct, we were in the locker room dressing and Murdock, with his usual tact and finesse, came stomping in. "I hear we got us another refugee from the Senior Center," he bellowed.

Vince had been getting dressed and was in his t-shirt. First, you have to understand that Vince is bald as a cue ball. Early in his career, he decided that with all his time spent in pools and showers, he just didn't want to screw around with taking care of hair, so he shaved it off. If he had a lollipop sticking out of his mouth, he would probably look like Kojak on Social Security.

Vince rose and turned to Murdock, his coachey muscles bulging under his t-shirt, and very calmly said, "Sir, if you have a problem with

Seniors why don't you just spit it out and let's get this settled once and for all."

Murdock took a look at Vince and stammered, "No, no problem. Just stay out of my way." And he stomped off to the other side of the room.

The encounter was not lost on the rest of the squad. Vince had made his chops.

The Captain introduced Vince to the squad and after the meeting he asked Ox, Vince and I to remain.

The Captain explained that he had a special assignment for Vince and me. The local BuyMart Mega-Store was experiencing an unusually high incidence of theft. Every retail store builds a loss or 'shrinkage' factor into their pricing. What that means is that they know they are going to get ripped off. They know that no matter what they do, a certain percentage of their merchandise is going out the door without being rung up. So, you and I, because we're honest, get to pay a higher price to underwrite the thieves.

Every large store has people on the payroll whose job is to discourage shoplifters. However, these are not trained security guards, they're just minimum wage folks walking around, hoping to spot someone stuffing a salami down their pants. And if they do catch someone, they have no authority to arrest. They can only try to detain the thief until the police arrive.

And the flip side of this coin is if they accuse someone of shoplifting and it turns out they're wrong, it's lawsuit city. So, too diligent you make mistakes and get sued. Too lax and the creeps walk away with the store. The typical damned if you do and damned if you don't scenario.

But lately, BuyMart was not just losing, they were hemorrhaging. Merchandise was disappearing at an alarming rate and they couldn't figure out how the perps were doing it.

Normally, this would be considered an internal security problem, but not in the case of BuyMart.

The owner of the national chain of BuyMarts, Dewey Coughlin, has friends in high places. Coughlin, with his innovative marketing plan, had become a millionaire and, to his credit, had become a philanthropist. He had created endowments to the arts and set up trust funds for college tuition for those who can't afford it, and made major contributions to the local hospital for a new wing.

These things do not go unnoticed at City Hall. Coughlin had called in some chits with the City Fathers and now we were about to be introduced to the BuyMart empire.

The reason Vince and I were chosen for the assignment was that we fit the demographic of a large percentage of BuyMart employees.

We were old.

Part of BuyMart's ingenious plan is to hire retired seniors. They work twenty to thirty hours a week and are therefore considered part time employees. Part time employees receive no overtime, medical or retirement benefits, so it's a great cost savings to the company. And the seniors don't care. They're already on Social Security and Medicare and twenty hours a week is as much as some of them can take AND, they're just grateful to have somebody that wants them and have a place to go.

Vince and I would blend in perfectly. Ox, not so much. Vince and I would be given assignments within the store and Ox was assigned patrol duty in the area surrounding the BuyMart Mega Store so he would be close by if we needed him.

Dewey Coughlin was a native of Arkansas and the national headquarters of the company is in Unionville, Arkansas. Coughlin was nothing, if not loyal to his roots, and many of his key employees were trusted friends from his days before he hit it big.

Gil Feeney, one of his Arkansas buddies from the old days, was the BuyMart store manager and, of course, he was in on the plan. Since no one had a clue where the theft was coming from, we were basically flying by the seat of our pants. The plan was to place Vince and I in varying positions throughout the store so that we could eventually take a look at all possible avenues of theft.

Our first day on the job was really special. We were given little BuyMart vests to wear over our shirts and a paper cap that read "BuyMart. If we haven't got it, you don't need it!"

Words to live by.

Vince was given a broom, mop and feather duster for light maintenance and I got to be the store 'greeter.' My job was to stand at the entrance, greet the shoppers coming in, give them a green sticker for any returned merchandise, and watch those exiting for any signs of shoplifting.

How hard can that be?

I took my position and as a scruffy guy in a dirty t-shirt and ponytail approached, I cheerfully said, "Good morning, Sir. Welcome to BuyMart."

As he passed, I heard his curt reply, "Kiss my ass!"

OK then, off to a rousing start.

Fortunately, most shoppers were polite or at least nodded in my direction.

A woman came in with a gallon milk jug with about two inches of milk left in the bottom. "Gotta return this," she said. "It's spoiled."

"No problem," I said, "just take it to the service desk down this aisle and they'll take care of you." But as I peeled off a green sticker and stuck it on the carton, I noticed the expiration date was two weeks ago.

"Ma'am," I said, "this milk expired two weeks ago."

"So what," she said and walked off toward the service desk.

Great scam, but what can you do? "The customer's always right." Right? I couldn't help but think how many honest milk sales it took to underwrite this blatant theft.

Then, over the intercom, I heard the announcement, "Vince, clean-up in aisle three." And I thought I had probably gotten the cushier job.

Later that morning, a young man in a wheelchair with a plaster cast on his leg was pushed in by his lady friend. I, of course, asked if there was anything we could do to make their shopping experience more pleasant. They said they were fine and picked up a small hand shopping basket and entered the store.

I had totally forgotten about them until they had gone through checkout and were exiting the building. Vince intercepted them at the door and asked to see their register receipt. He crosschecked the items in their bag with the receipt.

"Anything else you want to checkout before you leave?" He asked.

The guy shook his head and Vince reached down into the top of his cast and pulled out three Slim Jims, two Bic pens, and a Timex watch.

Vince showed his badge to the dismayed couple and called Ox on the walkie-talkies.

When Ox arrived, a smiling Vince put on his toughest face and ordered, "Book 'em, Dano!" As he walked by me he grinned, "I always wanted to say that!"

Nothing else memorable occurred the rest of the morning, and at noon I was relieved for a lunch break. I met Vince in the break room for a vending machine lunch.

He noticed me staring at some sticky goo on his pants and muttered, "Don't ask. Honey. Aisle three!"

We sat down at a long table with a couple of other guys, and Vince pulled his feather duster from his back pocket and laid it on the table.

That got the attention of one of our fellow diners. He looked at the fluffy duster and said to his buddy, "Ohhh, I'd like to take that home. I bet me and the old lady could have some fun."

"Gheeesh, Mitch," he replied. "What are you? Some kind of pervert?"

"Heck no," he retorted. "Using a feather is just kinky. A pervert would use the whole chicken." And he busted out laughing.

Backroom banter.

After lunch, I was taught to use the checkout register. You see? I'm moving up in the world. Vince was assigned to the fresh fruit and vegetable section. He was to pick out the items that had become too rotten to sell. I was starting to worry about Vince quitting. He seemed to be getting the crummy jobs.

Check out isn't so tough. You just slide the product over a glass screen, making sure the little code thingy is in the right position and 'beep,' it's rung up. A screen above the cash register and on the credit card reader identifies the item and the price. Isn't technology wonderful?

I was checking a lady with a huge basket of groceries and as I placed an enormous watermelon on the scanner, the screen read 'lemon ---$.50'.

" Wow!" I said. "That's one really big lemon!"

The woman never missed a beat, "Yeah," she replied. "I guess your stockers mislabeled it."

"Price check on register 12," I broadcasted over the intercom.

By the time I finished ringing up her basket, I had found six other 'mislabeled' items. Coincidence? I think not. These folks are really clever. They've figured out how to cheat the store, but left a way out if they get caught.

I quickly learned there are rules of etiquette at the check out stand. A robust woman had just emptied her cart on the checkout stand, but left two heavy containers of purified water in the cart. After I had checked everything but the water, I leaned over the counter and innocently said, "Ma'am, I 'd like to see your jugs." The look she gave me would have peeled paint. You gotta be careful what you say.

A middle-aged couple came through the line. The woman was pleasant looking, but her tummy definitely protruded. Wanting to bond with my customers, I said with a knowing smile on my face, "How soon is the baby due?"

The woman looked up horrified, burst into tears and ran out of the store.

I looked quizzically at her husband. He leaned over and whispered, "She ain't pregnant."

That evening, as I shared my day's events with Maggie, she informed me that you should NEVER, even remotely, suggest a woman is pregnant unless you can see her giving birth at that very moment.

Live and learn!

A guy came through with a piece of fruit that had no little sticker. Hoping to avoid a 'price check' wait, I queried the shopper, "Honeydew?" I asked.

He looked me in the eye and grinned as he replied, "Sometimes honey do and sometimes she don't."

Checkout humor.

Another guy, who looked a little 'swishy' came through the line. "Paper or plastic?" I asked.

He gave me a little wink as he replied, "Honey, I can go either way. I'm bi-sack-ual."

Just as I was about to complete my shift for the day, a really big woman with REALLY big breasts came through my line. Now you would expect a woman who tips the scales at about two-eighty, would have hefty knockers, but what was unusual was that these babies stuck straight out. I mean it looked like Madonna's ice cream cups on steroids.

Now I don't consider myself an expert in women's mammaries, but I am sixty-six years old, and in my experience, the breasts of women of this size would be called 'droopy' or 'saggy,' but never, ever, 'perky.'

As I was contemplating and staring, the woman piped up indignantly, "Hey, Buster, you staring at my boobs?"

"Yes, Ma'am," I replied. "I couldn't help but notice their perkiness."

"Pervert!" she screamed. "I want to see a manager."

When Gil walked up she bellowed, "This man was making sexual advances toward me. I wanna report him to the police."

Gil took a look at the big hooters pointed in our direction and said, "Walt, you think we can find this woman a cop?"

"Probably can." I replied, as I pulled my badge from my pocket.

We escorted our buxom belle to the back room where a female security girl found a pound of bacon tucked under each boob.

'Bringing home the bacon' suddenly had a new meaning.

When I returned to the checkout stand, another cashier had taken over my spot. "Walt," she said, "why don't you take over the express register on number three for the rest of your shift?"

So I did.

All was going well until I saw my dear old friend Mary approaching my register. "Hi, Mr. Walt," she exclaimed. "I want YOU to check me out."

As she was unloading her items on the counter, the man behind her was juggling a gallon of cold ice cream from hand to hand. He tapped her on the shoulder and said, "Lady, this is the express check out. Twelve items or less and I counted sixteen items in your basket."

"Oh, come on now," Mary replied. "You gonna bust my chops cause I put a couple extra boxes of Ex-Lax in my cart?"

"Rules are rules, Lady," he said. "You need to move to another line."

"OR WHAT?" she demanded. "You gonna report me to the mall cop?"

And I could see her face start to turn red.

The man was determined to stand his ground. "What's right is right," he said with an indignant look on his face.

The indignant look became one of fear as Mary put on her nasty face. "Mr. Walt," she said, "you better get this little prick outta my face before I do some rearranging on his!"

I was afraid I was going to have to arrest my old friend for assault and battery, when I noticed register two had opened up. "Sir," I said, "register two is open. We can help you over there."

A look of relief came over him. He hated to lose face, but he knew he had bit off more than he could chew. Tangling with Mary is kind of like playing football. You better know when to quit.

The next day, Vince got to stock shelves and I got to man one of the 'give away samples of stuff that we hope you will buy' displays.

My job was to cook little sausages in an electric fry pan, cut them in bite size pieces, stick little toothpicks in them, and beg people to taste them. Most people declined. Not that I blamed them. They looked like little boogers on a stick.

A man, dressed in a shirt and pants a size too large for him, came by and took the sample I offered. "Not bad," he said, "do you mind if I try another?"

"Nope, help yourself." And he left.

Another guy came by, grabbed a sausage and plopped it in his mouth. "Yuck," he said, "tastes like shit." And he spit it in the trashcan.

No accounting for taste.

Dolly was an aisle over, handing out samples of some kind of glop on a cracker. I noticed my baggy drawers guy was sampling her wares as well. "Try before you buy," I thought, but then I noticed that his cart was empty.

He disappeared around the corner.

After a couple of hours of sausage hawking, I needed a potty break, and I called Vince to relieve me so that I could relieve myself. When I returned, Mr. 'baggy breeches' was sampling sausages from Vince. It had been over an hour and his cart was still empty.

I approached and held up my badge and asked the man to accompany me into the break room. He hadn't broken any laws and I hadn't seen him pocket anything, but his behavior was definitely suspicious. Maybe he was casing the store.

In the back room, I sat him down. "OK, what's your story?" I asked.

The man seemed genuinely humiliated. He hung his head, told me how he had lost his job, his apartment and his self-respect. He was living on the street and was feeding himself by making the rounds of the grocery stores and other establishments handing out samples.

It certainly wasn't illegal and my heart ached for this once proud man who now had to grovel for his basic needs. I thought about all the lowlifes I'd seen that day, inventing ways to rip off the system, and here before me was a man ashamed at having to take a free sausage.

Lady Justice! We could use some help here.

I told him about the lunches at the Senior Center that were available for those who couldn't pay. I handed him a twenty, and as he shuffled off with bowed head, the old adage struck home, "There, but for the grace of God, go I."

Vince had been stocking shelves and was now working in my aisle. He was on a small three step stool stocking items on the top shelf.

As I was just getting ready to put another batch of sausages in the skillet, a woman in one of those handicapped scooters with the cart on the front came roaring around the corner. She barely missed me and my skillet of hot grease. Vince wasn't so lucky. As she blazed past him the wheel from the scooter caught the leg of Vince's ladder and he came down in a heap, and boxes of cake mix came crashing down on top of him.

I rushed to his side and when I saw that he wasn't hurt, the boxes of lemon chiffon and double chocolate covering him were just too much.

"You got something going on with Betty Crocker I don't know about?" I quipped.

He gave me an 'I'm gonna kick your ass' look and then we both burst into laughter.

We had just finished putting 'Betty' back in her place when "CODE 50" roared over the intercom.

Code 50 was used when a greeter had spotted a shoplifter and required assistance. We took off toward the front of the store.

The old gentleman who had spotted the thief was pointing down the fruit and vegetable aisle. "There! He's getting away!" he shouted.

We looked and saw the perp sprinting down the aisle toward the swinging door that ultimately led to the service entrance.

He was a good seventy-five feet from us when we spotted him. No way were we going to catch him before he made the swinging door. Vince grabbed a coconut from the fruit display and in one sweeping motion of that cannon arm, fired his fruit bomb at the perp. The coconut struck the fleeing felon squarely in the back of the head. He fell headlong into a display of picnic supplies and came down covered in plastic forks and paper plates.

"What an arm," I droned. "A great slide, but the runner is out at the plate."

Not bad for a day's work.

So far, we had exposed dirty tricks and petty thievery, but theft of this nature was to be expected and certainly didn't account for the massive losses the store was experiencing.

We gave our report to Gil and called it a day.

The next morning, I was back at greeter again. A woman approached me with a large box. "I bought this lap top computer, but when I opened the box there was nothing but this styrofoam and some wood."

"Hmmm," I thought. "Now were getting somewhere. We're not talking about a seventy-five cent Slim Jim. We're talking eight hundred bucks!"

I called someone to relieve me, took the lady for her refund and called a conference with Gil and Vince. After examining the box, we concluded that someone was tampering with the merchandise before it hit the floor. It had to be an inside job.

But from where?

All merchandise came from the main distribution center in Unionville, Arkansas, so, we concluded, that would be the logical place to start. If we could track a shipment from warehouse to store, we might be able to discover the culprit.

Vince and I met with the Captain and we had a conference call with Dewey Coughlin. He approved our plan and we made preparations for a field trip to Arkansas.

Coughlin told us to contact Larry Dugan when we arrived. Larry is in charge of the distribution center and another friend of Coughlin's from the old days. He said he would call Dugan and give him the details of our plan and assured us of full cooperation.

After our conference, Shorty asked me to stay behind. He said, "Walt, I'm afraid I have some bad news. We were all really excited about getting the C.R.A.P. program started, but we might have jumped the gun a bit. Captain Harrington, who, as you know, is not your biggest fan, went to the Executive Committee. He reminded them that each time a recruit is hired for your program that eliminates a new hire for the regular force. There is only so much money for salaries in the budget. I'm afraid they agreed with him. It looks like Vince may be it for quite awhile. I'm really sorry."

Yea, me too.

Naturally, I was discouraged. Why is it that so often new and innovative ideas are brought to a halt by mundane and practical realities?

Well, it is what it is, and Vince and I had a job to do.

It was a good six-hour drive from Kansas City to Unionville. We left early and arrived at the distribution center at three in the afternoon. We asked for Mr. Dugan and were sent to the loading dock.

We were met by three strapping men in overalls. The oldest approached with his hand extended. "Hi," he said. "My name's Larry and this is my brother Darryl and this here's my other brother, Darryl."

"No! It can't be," I thought. "That stuff only happens on TV."

But, this IS Arkansas.

We introduced ourselves and discussed the details of our plan.

"That all sounds good," he said. "But you boys barely caught us. We got us some big plans of our own for the evening. I'm going over to my brother-in-law's place. He just bought hisself a new house."

"Oh, kind of a house warming," I said.

"Yea, that too." Larry replied. "But mainly we got to help him take the wheels offn' it."

"Ahh," I said. "Then the Darryl's will be going with you."

"Nope, not tonight, they both got plans o' their own. Darryl here's got hisself a moon pie, a six-pack and a new bug zapper. He's looking forward to an evening of quality entertainment. And I saw Darryl over there with a new tub of lard."

"Oh, his wife must be planning on frying some chicken," I said.

"Nope," Darryl chimed in, "it's good for that too, but we use it mostly in bed."

Wow! Too much information.

There's obviously a lot I don't know about Arkansas culture.

"Yea, Darryl's feelin' a lot better since he came from the Doc this afternoon."

"Is Darryl ill?" I asked.

"Well, he thought he was. His wife told him he was gettin' Grapenuts and he thought he had one of them venereal diseases."

We bid the Dugan brothers farewell and checked into a local hotel. When we got in our room, we knew we had chosen first class accommodations. There was a stuffed possum on the dresser, a spit cup on the nightstand, three back issues of <u>Outdoor Life</u> on the coffee table and a velvet painting of Elvis on the wall. Arkansas luxury.

Our plan for the next day was fairly simple. An eighteen-wheeler was being loaded for the trip to the Kansas City BuyMart Mega Store. I, being the smaller of the two of us, was to be packed inside a large box that supposedly held a fifteen cubic foot refrigerator. Larry would see to it that I was loaded in the trailer at a location where I could see what was happening through little holes we had cut in the side of the box. Larry had inspected all of the shipment and so far, all the merchandise was intact. Vince would follow along at a safe distance in our car so as not to arouse suspicion.

BuyMart owns the trailers and they contract out for the drivers who own their rigs. The trailer was completely loaded and I was wheeled up the ramp in the big box. It was at least a six hour trip to Kansas City, so I had equipped myself with a couple of candy bars, a bottle of water and an empty bottle in case I had a call from mother nature.

We were all set. I heard the door slam shut and felt a jerk as the tractor hooked up to the trailer.

Off we go!

I had gone to the bathroom just before being sealed into the box, but with all the jiggling and bouncing, I soon was getting warning signals from my bladder. So there I was, sealed in a refrigerator box in the back of a truck, going seventy miles an hour down Highway 65, trying to piss in a Coke bottle. They just don't cover this stuff at the Academy.

After about an hour, I felt the big rig pull off the highway and on to a gravel road. It came to a stop and I heard voices. Then the door opened and as I peeped through my little holes, I saw the driver and another man take a box that contained a DVD player, open it, remove the DVD player and replace it with a block of wood the same size and weight as the player. They sealed the box and put it back with the other players.

Clever!

The number of boxes would match the invoice sheet. The DVD might sit in the warehouse for a month before it was put on the shelf, and might sit there several more weeks before someone bought it and returned it like the lady with the laptop.

Then they went to another box that contained maybe fifty watches. They carefully removed just one watch and sealed the carton. They only count cartons at check-in, not individual pieces. It would never be missed. These guys were good.

After pilfering several cartons, they slammed the door shut and I felt the trailer moving again.

There were no further incidents until we pulled into the loading dock at BuyMart.

When a trailer is unloaded, sturdy metal ramps with ball bearing wheels are placed on the back of the trailer and extend down into the warehouse. Boxes and crates are placed on the ramp, gravity takes over and the carton rolls into the waiting arms of the dockhand.

When I was in high school, I worked at the small town supermarket. It was the job of my buddy and I to unload the weekly grocery shipment. It became kind of a contest. The driver would load the cartons on the ramp and shoot them into the store as fast as he could. If we weren't there to catch them, they would go sailing off the end and crash onto the floor.

Great fun.

The driver opened the trailer door and with the help of the dock man, hoisted the ramps into place. Then he turned to the dock man and said he'd be back in a minute. I figured he was going to the bathroom and I would have plenty of time to cut myself out of the box.

I had just cut the top and was standing up when he returned. He must have just been getting a drink. When he saw me in the box, he knew he had been made. He pulled a gun from his pants. The startled dock man took off in the other direction. I scrambled out of the box just as he fired. A carton of mayonnaise exploded next to me. I ducked and his next shot took out Orville Redenbacher.

I felt like one of those ducks in a firing range at the carnival. I was trapped in the trailer and it was only a matter of time until one of his shots hit pay dirt.

Then I saw it. A large carton was on the edge of the ramp ready to be whizzed into the waiting arms of the loader. The driver was at the end of the ramp ready to fire again. I thought about how, as a kid, I would place my American Flyer sled at the top of a hill and with a running start, belly flop on the sled and speed down the hill.

What the hell! Either that or stay here and get shot.

I launched myself at the carton, hit it with a 'Whuff' and sped down the ramp with blazing speed. It all happened so quickly the driver didn't have time to react. He fired and I heard the bullet whiz over my head just as the carton and I struck him in the chest.

He collapsed in a heap and I cuffed him. I glanced at the box I had ridden in on and saw a mule on his front feet with his hind feet extended. The box label read "Louisana Ass-Kickin' Hot Sauce."

RIGHT ON!

Lady Justice! How does she do it?

I found Gil and he told me he had just gotten the report. Vince had seen the exchange between the two men and had followed the guy to the garage where they were hiding the contraband. He called it in and the State Highway Patrol came to assist in the collar.

Not a bad days work for a couple of old farts.

After the thieves were taken into custody and booked, Vince and I met with the Captain and through another conference call, shared with Dewey Coughlin how the perps were ripping off the company. He expressed his gratitude for our service and for the C.R.A.P. program and said he was in our debt. If there was anything he could ever do to square it up, just let him know.

The Captain thought for a minute and said, "Mr. Coughlin, by any chance are you looking for another worthy cause for an endowment?"

"We're always looking for a good tax write-off that will benefit the community," he replied. "What did you have in mind?"

The Captain explained our situation involving the suspension of the C.R.A.P. program, and before the morning was over, Dewey Coughlin had agreed to underwrite the expenses of the City Retiree Action Patrol.

How great is that!

Apparently Lady Justice does give a C.R.A.P.!

CHAPTER 24

I DROVE HOME HAPPY, but exhausted. I guess riding six hours in a box and getting shot at will take the starch out of a person.

As I walked up to my apartment building, Willie was sitting on the front porch reading my newspaper.

"Hey, Mr. Walt," he said, "Mary tells me you workin' down at de BuyMart. I been meaning to get me some stuff, you know, stuff to take care of the ladies. You suppose you could get me one o' dem employee discounts?"

"Sorry, Willie," I replied. "My BuyMart days are over. I turned in my cap and vest."

"Damn," he said. "Emma's been wanting to see me, but even at my age, I can't go ridin' into de sunset witout my hat on."

Good to know Willie practices safe sex.

The Professor once told us: "You should wear a condom on every conceivable occasion."

I glanced over Willie's shoulder at the front-page headline. It read, "Importer Myron Blanchard Found Hanged. Suicide Suspected." The article went on to say that Blanchard was found by an employee at one of Blanchard's import warehouses in the West Bottoms. He was found hanging by a rope from a ceiling rafter. The room was empty except for an overturned chair.

I had read about Blanchard and his partner, Clark Grissom. They were up and comers in Kansas City commercial circles. Their imports from East Asian and European markets were filling the shelves on Midwest retail stores. Makes you wonder why such a successful guy would pull the plug.

Willie said, "Mr. Walt, Mary called and wanted me to come over and replace some light bulbs in de hall what she couldn't reach. You got time to take me ova der?"

I looked at my watch. "Still early. Why not?" And we headed to The Three Trails.

Mary was headed out the door when we arrived. "Hey, Mr. Walt," she said, "I was just heading to the downtown bus stop. Gotta go see about a cataract."

"Whoa," Willie chimed in, "wot's an old lady like you need wit a big ole car like dat?"

"Not a Cadillac, you dipshit," she replied. "A cataract. You know, in my eye."

"Oh yea," Willie said, "I knew dat."

Sure.

"Tell you what," I said, "let's get those light bulbs changed and I'll drive you downtown. You won't have to wait for the bus."

So Willie finished his chores and as we headed downtown, Mary remarked, "Mr. Walt, since I don't have to wait for the bus, I've got some extra time. My tummy's been growling at me. You think we might stop at a drive-thru and pick up a sandwich?"

I hadn't eaten much myself and Willie's always hungry so we pulled into the first drive-thru we found.

I pulled into the drive-thru lane and inched my way closer to the order speakerphone. As I rolled my window down, a muffled voice came from the speaker, "Mlunth drsjp?"

Having been through drive-thrus before, I figured that was speaker ease for "May I take your order?"

"Yes." I yelled into the speaker. "We'd like three Mega Burgers, no onions, fries, two Cokes and a coffee, black."

"Tufhsk leabn," came the reply.

"Oh yea," Mary said, "give me one of those little apple pies, too."

"Beavun yusfh," was all I heard.

I saw the amount of the bill registered on the digital readout by the speaker and it looked about right, so I pulled through to the pickup window.

The window flew open. I looked up and 'YIKES!' The girl at the window looked like she had lost a fight with a nail gun. Each ear was pierced three times and each hole was adorned with large hoop earrings. There was a stud bar through her eyebrow, a diamond stud on her left nostril, and two studs protruding from her lower lip. When she opened her mouth to speak, her tongue flopped out sporting a stud the size of a pea.

"No wonder the girl can't talk." Mary said. "Her mouth's stapled shut."

I handed her a twenty and tried not to think about the fact that the food I was about to eat had been prepared by a practitioner of self-mutilation.

I pulled out of the line and into traffic. Mary was opening the sack of goodies and distributing the food when I heard her exclaim, "Oh Crap! That little bitch put onions on my burger. I didn't want to go to no doctor breathing onions up his nose."

I turned to calm her down and when I looked up again, the car in front of me had stopped to make a left turn. I jammed on my brakes just as Willie was peeling the lid off his coffee.

The coffee sloshed out and Willie screamed, "YEOW! I done scalded my pecker!" and he began frantically undoing his pants. "Ice, Ice," he shouted, "gimme some ice!"

Mary poured what was left of her coke out the window and turned to hand Willie the ice and saw, I presume for the first time, Willie's manhood, as he frantically wiped it with a napkin.

"Holy shit," she exclaimed. "You steal that thing off a mule?"

"Ohhh," moaned Willie, "now I can't go see Emma fo at least a week!"

My life is nothing, if not exciting.

I delivered Mary to her eye doctor and drove Willie home. He was still complaining about his affliction when we met the Professor.

After hearing Willie's tale of woe, he helped put everything in perspective: "It's better to have a diamond with a flaw than a pebble without."

And Willie went away happy.

The next morning after squad meeting, the Captain asked me to stay behind. He handed me an envelope that was addressed to "Walter Williams, c/o C.R.A.P. Program."

"Looks like you've got a fan," the Captain said.

I opened the envelope that contained a computer-generated message which read:

"A dead man is found in a locked room, hanging from the ceiling four feet above the floor. The room is completely empty, except for a puddle of water below him. How did he die?"

We stared at the note. "What the hell is this, Walt?" he asked.

"Don't have a clue." I replied. The note was not signed and the envelope had no return address.

"Why would someone send a riddle to the police department?" He queried.

Riddle!

Of course, the first thing that popped into my pitiful mind was Batman and his relationship with the evil Riddler of Gotham City. I decided against mentioning that to the Captain.

But then something else clicked. "I saw a death by hanging in the paper yesterday," I said, "Myron Blanchard."

"Yes, but the coroner has ruled that as a suicide." He said. "The only thing in the room was a chair that he probably stood on, then kicked away. There was no evidence of foul play."

I looked at the riddle again. "Did they find a puddle of water below him?" I asked.

"Hmmm, I don't recall anything like that in the report, but I'll check with the officers on the scene." He replied. "Better leave this note with me until we can figure out what's going on."

"Any chance I could take a look at the scene?" I asked. "I'm sure the first officers didn't miss anything, but with this note, I'd like to take a look around."

"Sure," he replied.

So, Ox and I headed for the West Bottoms and I told him about the note.

The scene of the hanging was an old storage warehouse that was part of the Overseas Exports complex. It was several blocks away from the main office and according to the initial report it was seldom used. Empty, secluded, sparingly used. A perfect location for a suicide -----or a murder.

We entered the room and found it exactly as had been described in the report. It was totally empty except for the overturned chair. The ceiling rafters were at least ten feet above the floor and could not have been reached with just a chair. A ladder would have been needed, but where was the ladder?

We studied the riddle and compared it to the room. There were discrepancies. The riddle described a locked room. The crime scene door was unlocked. The riddle said the room was empty. The crime scene had a chair. The riddle had a puddle of water under the victim. The crime scene had a ------ DRAIN!

"Let's pretend the crime scene is like in the riddle," I said. "Maybe the note is trying to tell us to look beyond the physical evidence. If the door is locked, then no one but the victim could have been present. If there is no chair or ladder, how did the victim get enough height to hang himself? And what's with the water? Where did that come from?"

"Maybe his bladder let loose when he died," Ox offered.

"The riddle doesn't say urine and even if it was, that doesn't solve the other two puzzles." I replied.

"OK, where can water come from?" I asked. "There's no water source in the room. There's no container that could have held the water. Where else can water come from?"

"Ice is water," Ox said.

"Well, yea!" I exclaimed. "Ice is solid water. Solid means you could stand on it. You could get high enough above the floor so that when the ice melted, you would have no footing and strangle. Let's apply that theory to our crime scene."

"A large block of ice is brought into the room. The rope is hung from the rafter. The victim is placed on the ice. The ice melts and the victim strangles, but in our scene the water disappears down the drain and leaves no evidence." I said.

"If he's on a block of ice, what's with the chair?" Ox asked.

I thought for a minute. "The chair is to make it look like a suicide. No ice, just an overturned chair. It's what you would find at most suicide scenes."

"The guy's hands weren't tied," Ox said. "If they leave him just standing there on the ice, what's to keep him from untying the rope."

"He must have been unconscious," I replied. "In obvious suicides, where the cause of death is strangulation, they don't perform complete autopsies. I'd be willing to bet they will find something in his blood stream that put him out."

"Damn!" Ox muttered. "We got us a murder!"

I took a photo of the floor drain with my cell phone and we hotfooted it back to the precinct to tell the Captain our theory.

"Sounds like a stretch to me," he said. "Only one way to find out." He called the morgue and ordered a complete autopsy including a tox screen. "We'll know something tomorrow," he said. "And if your theory is correct, who sent this riddle and how did they know?"

Good question.

The next day, the tox screen came back with evidence that Blanchard had chloroform in his system. It was enough for the Captain to re-open the case, and the headline in the newspaper that evening read: "Police Re-open Blanchard Case. Evidence Points To Murder, Not Suicide."

The next morning the Captain called me aside again. Another letter had been sent to the station addressed to me.

The note inside read: "Good work, Walter. Now follow this clue. 'He who has it doesn't tell it. He who takes it, doesn't know it. He who knows it, doesn't want it.' Good luck."

"Good grief!" Shorty said. "Now what? Why can't they come right out and tell us what they want us to know? Why all the mystery?"

"Well, one thing is certain," I replied. "They want to remain anonymous. I think someone is trying to point us in the right direction without implicating themselves. Maybe they're afraid if they come forward, it would put them in danger."

"I think you're on the right track, Walt," He replied. "We'll get this note to the Detectives and see what they make of it."

The rest of the day was routine police work.

When I returned home that evening, I poured a glass of Arbor Mist and plopped down on my porch swing. There's something about those old swings hanging from the ceiling on chains that just seem to take the wrinkles out of a day. I have found that I do some of my best thinking just sitting there, going back and forth, with my feet dangling down.

It wasn't long before I was joined by the Professor and Willie. Oh well, so much for peace, quiet and contemplation. I figured that since my private meditation had been disrupted, I might as well share our riddle with my friends. So I got two more glasses and shared my Arbor Mist. Sometimes, just bouncing ideas around with others brings out a point of view you would not have seen by yourself.

After I read the riddle and put it in the context of the murder, we all fell silent as we tried to find an explanation.

Willie spoke first. "I got it!" he exclaimed. "It's de clap! I had de clap once. And if you got it you sho don't tell no one. If you get it, you sho don't know it tell your pecker starts burnin'. And if you got it, you sho don't want it." He beamed with pride.

The Professor and I looked at each other. "Well," I said, "it certainly does fit the clues, but I'm not sure how it would fit into our case. We'll keep it in mind, but maybe we should keep on thinking."

Willie was crestfallen. He had the clap for nothing.

The Professor spoke. "I think the key is, 'He who 'takes' it'. In Willie's example and in any transmitted disease, you don't 'take it', you 'get it'. It's transmitted, not actually received. I think we're talking about some tangible, physical object that can be passed from hand to hand."

"OK," I said. "If you have it and you know there's a problem with it, you don't admit it. You give it to someone, but they don't know it has a problem. And if they find out about the problem, they want to get rid of it."

I remembered an old Arthur Godfrey tune from back in the fifties. It was called "The Thing." It was about a guy walking along the beach who found a box. He opened it up and the song says he found a 'Boom, Boom, Boom.' He tried every way in the world to get rid of it, but nobody would take it. The song, of course, never said what it was.

My mind is filled with useless information.

"Try this," I said. "A guy is selling apples. He finds an apple with a worm. He doesn't tell it. Instead he puts it in the bottom of a basket of good apples. A guy comes along and buys the basket of apples, but he doesn't know there's one in the bottom with a worm. He gets home, takes the apples from the basket and finds the one with the worm. Of course, he doesn't want it. But like Willie's clap, it fits the clues, but doesn't really fit in our case."

"I think you're on the right track," the Professor said. "Now, we just have to find some physical object that makes sense within the context of your case."

We thought some more.

"Maybe it has to do with the products they import," the Professor said. "What if someone purchased an expensive collector's item and found out it was a knock off?"

"Hmmm, don't think that fits either," I said. "First, Overseas Exports doesn't deal in collectables. Everything they buy is mass-produced. It's all junk to start with and the retailers know what they're getting. And

139

if someone thought they were being ripped off, why not just sue? Why concoct such an elaborate scheme to kill the guy?"

"How 'bout dis?" Willie asked. "Back in de day, when I was boostin' stuff, I had dis nice little TV set. I sold it to a guy who paid me wif a rubber check. He knowed it was bad when he give it to me. I sho didn't know it was bad when I took it and I sho didn't want it when I found out. I had to go thump on the guy to get my money."

From the mouths of babes!

"That's it!" The Professor and I shouted at once. "Not checks, but counterfeit money!"

An import/export business is the perfect place to launder funny money. It was possible that something went wrong with the scheme and someone was cleaning up loose ends.

I couldn't wait to get to the station to share our idea with the Captain. He thought the idea had merit, but to his knowledge, there had been no reports of counterfeit money being spread around the city.

Then, a thought occurred to him. Unfortunately, within our government bureaucracy, sometimes the right hand doesn't tell the left hand what's going on. A counterfeit investigation would normally be under the jurisdiction of the Treasury Department. And more times than not, the Feds don't share.

This was bigger than Shorty could handle, so he took it to the Chief. The Chief made a call to the Federal Building and the Treasury boys grudgingly admitted they were investigating a counterfeit ring.

BINGO!

The Chief told the Feds about the riddles and our theory how they connected, and a joint task force was set up to investigate the murder/counterfeit operation.

I felt kind of torqued. A major crime investigation was underway as a direct result of three old friends sitting on a porch, sharing a glass of Arbor Mist and shooting the bull.

CHAPTER 25

THE ENTIRE SQUAD WAS GATHERED for the morning briefing when Captain Short entered the room.

He briefed us on the joint task force and assigned several officers to participate. I was disappointed that Ox and I weren't invited.

Then he said, "Gentlemen, we're going to be conducting an undercover sting operation and we need a volunteer." He turned to me and said, "Why, thank you, Walt, for volunteering."

I didn't remember raising my hand. "Exactly what did I just volunteer for?" I asked.

"A prostitution ring is operating in the Downtown area," he said. "We think it's coming from the Red Garter Club. We need to have you frequent the Club, and see if you can get one of the girls to solicit you."

"Why me?" I asked.

"Because you fit the demographic for the typical 'john'. There are two types of guys who use the strip clubs for their jollies, blue-collar workers and seniors. It's the perfect place if you're looking for a good time on a limited budget. The wealthy don't need strip clubs. If you've got the dough, you can find action at less public places."

"OK, so I'm a senior. Why not get one of the younger guys to be a construction worker?" I asked.

"Well, Walt, you sort of fit the other demographic we're looking for," he said.

"Oh really? And what would that be?" I asked.

"Well, you look sort of -------- ummm, needy," he replied.

"NEEDY!" Just what every guy wants to hear. "What about Vince?" I asked. "He's old too."

"Yea, but Vince looks like he could go out and get anything he wants," he replied. And a muffled giggle spread throughout the room.

"Wonderful," rub salt in the wound.

"Gosh, I don't know." I said. "Maggie's been real good about all this so far, but I don't think she's going to be real excited about me going to a strip club."

Maggie was OK with me getting punched, pummeled and shot, but this is a whole different deal.

Women have a tendency to get their panties in a wad if they catch you looking around. Now, I'm certainly no prude, and I have trouble with the clerics preaching hell, fire and brimstone. It's one of those things you have to take on faith.

I'm more of a practical guy, and I'm scared shitless of the old 'hell hath no fury like a woman scorned.' I have seen friends and acquaintances emasculated, both emotionally and financially, by vindictive females. I want no part of that action!

Besides, I love Maggie and I would never hurt her. I never want the old country song, "A good hearted woman in love with a good timin' man" to apply to us.

"Maggie will understand," the Captain said. "Besides, it's your job."

It turned out that my job was to patronize the Red Garter, poke some dollar bills in some G-strings, buy a few lap dances and hope I look 'needy' enough that one of the girls in the prostitution ring will offer her services.

I have to stay undercover until money changes hands, at which time I would say the code sentence, "I need to go to the bathroom first," and the guys listening to me through my wire will pop in for the bust.

All in a day's work.

Of course, the next day, Maggie called and wanted to get together after work. I told her I was going to be busy the next few evenings in an undercover operation. When she wanted details, I told her it was a sensitive operation that I wasn't at liberty to discuss.

Not exactly a lie. It definitely was going to be sensitive. I just didn't realize how sensitive until I got involved.

We were all set up. I had put on my 'needy' clothes and the wire was taped in place. I was given a wad of dollar bills and three hundred dollars in twenty's. Ox and Vince were in the black and white a block away, listening.

Another reason I never patronized these establishments was the economics involved. Lap dances cost twenty bucks each and last a whole three minutes. That's roughly twenty dances an hour. Four hundred bucks! Do the math. The only other place it costs that much to get screwed is your lawyer's office.

I'd much rather spend the money on a nice evening out with Maggie, even if I do have to tip Rolph.

I walked in the Red Garter and my ears were assaulted by the 'THUMP, THUMP, THUMP', of the bass on the song currently blasting at approximately the decibel level of a jet engine. A scantily clad young lady was on stage gyrating to the music, and other girls were busy grinding away on needy laps.

I looked around the room and figured I must be lost. I thought silicone valley was in California. I had definitely landed in 'perky city.'

Prior to entering the establishment, I had a conversation with Mr. Winkie, and explained, as forcefully as I could, that we were on a work assignment and that he was to behave himself. To my dismay, I realized Mr. Winkie had a mind of his own.

It brought to mind a Robin Williams' quote: "God gave men both a penis and a brain, but unfortunately, not enough blood supply to run both at the same time."

Control, control.

I took a seat at the stage just as the next dancer appeared. It's amazing what sometimes pops into your mind out of nowhere. I suddenly thought of Elvis in the movie <u>Roustabout</u> where he sings, "I went and bought myself a ticket and sat down in the very first row. Little Egypt came out struttin' wearing nuttin' but a button and a bow."

And here she was.

I watched the other guys for a few minutes and realized there is certain etiquette in garter stuffing. If you want a closer look, you hold up your dollar and Ms. Wiggles comes over, gives you a close up, and you deposit the bill in her garter or G-string. I finally found the courage to hold up a dollar and, sure enough, it worked.

After awhile a girl came up and sat beside me. "Hey there big boy," she purred. "Is that a gun in your pocket or are you just glad to see me?"

Mae West humor.

Actually, it was my roll of dollar bills, but I let her think what she wanted.

"How about a dance, Sweetie," she whispered in my ear.

"Ohhhh Boy! Remember, it's just a job. For the good of the city. Civic duty, and all that."

She led me to a chair in the back of the room and the Rolling Stones "I Can't Get No Satisfaction" started playing. I hoped that would be the case.

I had read about prisoners of war suffering intense interrogation and torture. They survived by focusing their minds on pleasant thoughts of home. As Ms. Wiggles gyrated on my lap, I thought of Maggie.

The evening progressed and I alternated between the stage and the chair. Suddenly the lights flashed off and on, the music stopped and the bartender announced over the intercom, "All right, Gentlemen, this is the moment you have been waiting for. The Red Garter is proud to present our feature attraction, The Amazing Electra." And a round of applause echoed through the room.

A fanfare blared, the music started and out came Electra. 'YIKES!' She had long, coal black hair flowing over her shoulders and black eye shadow and liner so thick it must have been applied with a spoon. She wore black pasties and a black leather G-string that left little to the imagination and she wore a studded black leather collar around her neck. And to top it off, she carried a whip! If Lily Munster had been re-incarnated as a stripper, this would be her.

Now as I said before, I'm no prude, but I've never understood this 'S&M' punishment stuff. To me lovemaking should be sweet and tender and certainly not involve pain. But who am I to judge others. Remember, I'm the guy who thinks Arbor Mist is a fine wine.

The Amazing Electra began her act and right away I could see she had developed a special talent. Instead of guys poking dollars in her G-string, they would hold them up by the tip and Electra would snatch them out of their fingers with a flick of her whip.

One poor sap apparently had consumed more alcohol than he should have for this exercise and just as Electra cracked her whip toward his outstretched dollar he swayed ever so slightly and the whip caught him around the wrist. He yelped in pain and a roar went up from the other spectators.

Ouch! That's going to leave a mark!

Electra was definitely the highlight of the evening. I decided on one more lap dance before I hit the road. A young lady approached me for my last dance and I had a sudden urge, so I said, "Be right back. I need to go to the bathroom first." As I headed to the can, I heard sirens blaring up the street. "Oh Crap! Abort, Abort," I whispered into my mike. "False alarm. I really do need to take a leak." To my relief, the sirens stopped.

My evening at the Red Garter ended. I had put eighteen dollars in G-strings and spent eighty dollars on lap dances but had received no solicitations. Oh well, it's the city's money.

Since I was working evenings, I didn't have to report to the precinct until three in the afternoon. I gave Maggie a call. One advantage of dating a realtor is that they have no set work hours, and for the most part, can set their own schedules. Maggie had no appointments that morning so I asked if we could get together. I told her this undercover job was really stressful and asked if we could 'unwind' together. It would be a real help. To her credit, Maggie knew just how to help me unwind. Without realizing it, she had made a significant contribution to an ongoing police investigation. Mr. Winkie is a lot easier to control if he is Mr. Happy instead of Mr. Needy.

It's a guy thing.

That evening was pretty much the same as the night before. More G-strings and lap dances. I had been there about two hours when I was approached by a cute blond. "Looking for a dance?" she asked.

"Sure, why not?" I replied.

After the dance, instead of trotting off after another sucker, she whispered. "I saw you here last night. Are you in town for a convention?"

"No, I was just feeling kinda lonely. Didn't know where else to go." I replied in my most needy voice.

"I think I might have something that will make you feel better," she purred.

"What have you got in mind?" I asked

"I get off at eleven," she whispered. "Meet me at the Drake Hotel, room 213, and I can make you feel real good."

"I don't know," I said. "I don't have a lot of cash and besides, I've never done anything like that before."

Innocent, but true.

"I can make you real happy for two hundred," she said.

So we made the deal.

I hung around a few minutes more and left the Red Garter. I found Ox and Vince a block away. "Hey, Walt," Vince crowed, "I was beginning to feel sorry for you myself. The Captain sure picked the right guy."

"All an act." I replied.

We went over our plan and waited for eleven o'clock to arrive.

I knocked on the door and Blondie invited me in. She was all business. "Whatcha lookin' for?" she asked.

"Well —uhh--, like I told you, I've never done this before. Help me out," I replied. I could imagine Ox and Vince rolling their eyes.

"Straight sex, nothing kinky, two hundred bucks," she said.

"Sounds good to me," I replied.

"OK then, let's take care of business first," she said. And I pulled the wad of twenty's out of my pocket.

She took the money and stashed it in her purse. As she started unbuttoning her blouse, I said, "Hang on a minute. I have to go to the bathroom first."

The moment the sentence came out of my mouth, Ox and Vince broke through the door.

After they cuffed her and Mirandized her, she turned to me and said, "You're a cop? But you're so old!"

HA! Fooled You!

The brass at the station were delighted we had made a 'bust', so to speak. But they were after bigger fish. After interrogating Blondie, they offered her a deal. Give up the name of the ringleader in return for a reduced sentence. She bought it.

It was no surprise that the head of the prostitution ring was The Amazing Electra. She had four of the Red Garter girls beside herself turning tricks. She's the one we wanted. You want to kill a snake, you cut off its head.

Blondie had to play along with us to set the trap. She would normally meet with Electra the next day to hand over her share of the money. We gave Blondie the two hundred bucks and her job was to let Electra know that her john from the previous night was looking for some S&M, her specialty. She gave us the names and descriptions of the other three girls in the ring and we were ready to take them down.

I entered the club about nine o'clock. Ox and Vince were waiting outside and at my signal they would enter and take custody of the other three girls. Electra was all mine.

Blondie sat down beside me and whispered that everything was set. After Electra's number, I was supposed to follow her into her dressing room and she would take care of me there. The price was four hundred dollars.

'CRIPES.'

"Who pays four hundred dollars to get their butt whipped? My Mom used to do it for free!" I had to make a trip outside and get some extra cash from the boys.

Electra came onstage and began her act. She saw Blondie sitting next to me and that was her signal. She whipped the dollar out of the guy's hand sitting next to me and gave me a wink. So we were on.

After her show, I followed her to her dressing room and knocked. She opened the door, pulled me in and threw me on the bed. "I hear you've been a VERY BAD BOY!" she growled.

"Excuse me?" I said. Then I remembered why I was there. "Yes ma'am," I muttered. "Really Bad. I need to be punished."

"Electra can hurt you bad," she snarled. "But let's take care of business first."

As she advanced toward me in her leather and studded collar, I wasn't the least bit turned on. Frightened, yes! Turned on, definitely not!

I pulled the money out of my pocket and she tucked it away in her purse. Then she turned toward me with a pair of handcuffs and said, "All right, you naughty boy. Come to Electra."

For the life of me, I can't imagine guys going for this.

"Uhhh, hang on a minute," I said, "I need to go to the bathroom first."

As soon as I said it, we heard commotion in the bar. A red light came on by her dresser. The bartender had signaled that a raid was going on.

She turned to me with a genuine mean look in her eyes. "You're a damn cop," she sneered. "I should've known an old fart like you wouldn't want what I've got to give." And she pulled a .32 out of her purse.

I ducked as a shot rang out and shattered the mirror over the dressing table behind me.

I frantically looked around the room for a place to hide or something to protect myself with or ANYTHING.

How do I get into these jams?

Then I saw it on the bed where she had dropped it. The whip! Immediately visions of Lash LaRue and more recently, Indiana Jones, popped into mind, and I could see myself lash out and rip the gun out of her hand.

I grabbed the whip, but on its back lash, it wrapped around a vase of flowers and as I whipped my arm forward, I could feel the 'Whoosh' of air as the vase flew by my head and struck Electra right in her studded collar.

'OUCH.' It didn't come out exactly like I had envisioned it, but the end result was the same.

Sometimes it's better to be lucky than good.

Lucky!

I reached into my pocket and felt my buckeye from Gordon's Orchard.

"Luck?" I wondered, or something else?

Electra fell in a heap. I cuffed her and said, "Electra, you've been a very bad girl. Now Walt's going to have to punish you."

A passage from the Bible came to mind, "As ye sow, so shall ye reap."

Lady Justice knows her scripture.

And with that, we wrapped up the Red Garter Gang.

CHAPTER 26

IT HAD TAKEN US three days to take down the Red Garter gang. I was anxious to hear what progress had been made in the Riddler case. I was disappointed to discover that there had been very little.

Since the import company was owned by Blanchard and his partner, Clark Grissom, the detectives naturally wanted to talk to Grissom. Unfortunately, he had not been seen since the day of Blanchard's death. His wife, Laura, said he never returned home after work that evening, and he had not contacted her. A BOLO was issued for Grissom.

Further questioning of both Laura Grissom and the employees at the company verified that Mrs. Grissom was not directly involved in the day-to-day business of the company.

The powers at City Hall had tried to keep the formation of the joint task force quiet, but, as usual, someone leaked it to the press. Soon the whole city knew we were trying to connect Blanchard's murder with a counterfeit/money laundering operation.

The day I returned, another letter was addressed to me at the station. I opened it and we all read: "Good job, Walter. I knew you could figure it out. Figure this out and you'll have your next clue. 'Give me food and I will live. Give me water and I will die.' Good luck."

We just stared at each other. Here we go again.

"This one seems a lot easier," I said. "There are thousands of things that grow when you feed them, but how many things die when you give them water?"

"How about a fire?" Ox said, "It seems to fit. You give it fuel or food and it burns, but if you give it water, it dies."

"For want of something better, let's go with that for now." The Captain said, "You two contact the city fire department and check on all the fires since Blanchard's death and see if anything fits."

We went to the headquarters building of the Fire Department. They keep a record of all fires to which they respond, on a main computer terminal. It had been five days since Blanchard's death and thirty-two fires were logged during that time period.

We sat down at the terminal and started reviewing the details of each fire. It was a list of the usual: kitchen grease fires, leaf burning that had gotten out of control and a couple of automobiles that had been torched.

Then we saw a small warehouse building in the East Bottoms that had been completely destroyed by fire. It wasn't an expensive building. There was no insurance on the structure and there were no signs of an accelerant, so the fire marshal had ruled out arson. The legal owner of record was listed in the report.

Guess who? Myron Blanchard!

There is no program that cross references routine fires with ongoing criminal investigations, and no one, so far, had connected the fire with the dead importer.

We took down the address of the warehouse on North Garfield in the Bottoms and headed that direction.

The building was, of course, just a pile of rubble. The fire had been three days ago, so all the heat had dissipated. Since Blanchard was dead, no one had started cleanup. The site was just as the firemen had left it.

We started wading and rummaging through the soggy mess. We found mostly charred wood, several stacks of paper tied in bundles that had only burnt on the outside, and the twisted metal of what appeared to be some kind of press machine.

"By golly, Ox," I said. "I think we may have found where they were printing the money."

In a counterfeiting operation, the most important ingredient is the engraving plates. Presses can be replaced and more paper can be bought, but a good set of plates is worth their weight in gold. We searched the rubble in vain, looking for the plates, but as I suspected, someone removed the plates before torching the building and destroyed the evidence.

We were busy digging when I saw a black SUV swerve around the corner in our direction. I didn't pay much attention until I saw the back window go down and an AK-47 aimed in our direction.

I shouted at Ox who hadn't seen the vehicle. I tackled him to the ground as the AK-47 opened fire and a hail of bullets whizzed over our heads. We drew our weapons, but the SUV continued on down the block and out of sight.

"I think we may be on the right track," I said. "Looks like we're bringing the bad guys, whoever they are, out of the woodwork."

Unfortunately, it happened so fast, we didn't get a license number. We reported back to the Captain and he sent a forensics team to the site to gather any evidence the fire didn't destroy.

Shot at again. This is really getting old. Or is it me that's getting old? Naw. Bring it on!

I clocked out and headed home. As I approached my building, Bernice Crenshaw, my eighty-five year old tenant from 2-B was wandering around the yard.

"Oh, Mr. Walt," she lamented, "I'm so glad you're here. I've been looking all over for my Sunday paper. Did you happen to see it this morning as you left? I bet some creep stole it."

"Uhh, Bernice," I replied, "this is just Saturday. Your Sunday paper won't be delivered until tomorrow."

She paused for a moment as the information sunk in, then exclaimed, "Well shit, ---that's why no one was at church today!"

After her initial outburst of indignation, she just kind of sagged, and a tear welled up in her eye. "I just don't know what I'm going to do," she wailed. "I'm getting worse all the time. I lock myself out of my apartment. I go to the refrigerator and open the door and don't remember what I was going to get, and now I don't even know what day it is. Pretty soon my kids are going to put me in one of those homes. I just can't bear the thought."

"Oh, I think you've got a little time left," I said. "After all, you've got me and Willie and the Professor here to make sure you don't get in too much trouble."

She perked up a bit at that. Then she pulled a clipping from a magazine out of her pocket. "I found this today and I'm going to tape it on my bathroom mirror because it's just the way I feel." And she handed me the clipping. It read:

The Golden years are here at last.

I cannot see, I cannot pee.

I cannot chew, I cannot screw.

My memory shrinks, My hearing stinks.

No sense of smell, I look like hell.

The Golden Years have come at last.

The Golden Years can kiss my ass!

OK, I can relate to some of that.

"Bernice," I said, "you got anything going right now?"

"Don't think so," she replied, "but how the hell would I know?"

"Tell you what," I said. "I've kind of got a sweet tooth. How about you and me walking down to the Dairy Bar for a soda? You up for a date?"

"You bet," she replied. And we were off.

We walked to the Dairy Bar a block away, perched on the stools at the counter and ordered two chocolate sodas.

We had just got our sodas when an elderly gentleman walked in. We watched him and with a great deal of effort and obvious pain, he hoisted himself up on a stool. He was still grimacing when the waitress took his order.

"I'll have a banana split," he ordered.

"Crushed nuts?" she asked.

"Naw, just arthritis," he replied.

Glad we got that cleared up.

As we slurped our sodas, we noticed the old gentleman glancing our way with his eye on Bernice. Finally, he said, "Hi. My name's Carl. You come here often?"

Octogenarian pick-up line.

Bernice looked at me and said, "I can't remember. Walt, do I?" And so began a conversation between Bernice and Carl that ended with me being jilted by an old guy with arthritis.

After I paid our ticket, Carl told me I could be excused and he would walk Bernice home. So I wrote her address on a piece of paper, handed it to Carl, and made a hasty exit.

I guess there's someone for everyone.

As I was leaving for work the next morning, I met Bernice in the hall.

"How did it go with Carl?" I asked.

She looked at me and actually blushed, "I think it went really well. He walked me home, I invited him in, and we had sex."

Oh good grief! I didn't need to know that!

"It was a little embarrassing," she said. "After it was over, he said if he knew I was still a virgin, he wouldn't have been so rough with me. I told him that was OK. If had known he could really get it up, I would have taken off my pantyhose."

Seniors have a whole set of problems of their own.

I drove to the precinct and checked in for squad meeting. In his briefing, Captain Short announced that we were making some progress in the Riddler case. Forensics did determine that the burned warehouse was where the funny money was being printed. Both presses and paper were identifiable but, as suspected, no engraving plates were found.

Blanchard's ownership of the warehouse provided the link we needed to confirm that the murder and the counterfeiting were connected.

We were speculating as to the identity of the thugs that had shot at us, when an officer appeared with a letter. The Captain looked at it and handed it to me. Another note from the Riddler.

We opened it and it read:

"Good job, Walter. Now, if you want to know who shot at you, solve this riddle. 'What's black and white and red all over? 9/6, B-2.' Good luck."

This one had us baffled. We studied it for a while and finally decided to let it percolate in our minds. And we were off for our daily rounds.

When I returned home that evening, Willie was waiting for me. "Ole Mary's needin' us agin," he said. "She think Billy Bob in #9 done snuck in a pet, but he won't open de door fo' her."

Oh great!

I have a strict 'no pets' policy in my buildings. In thirty years as a landlord, I have seen it all. In addition to the normal dogs, cats, and birds, tenants have sneaked in hamsters, mice, tarantulas, pythons, iguanas and one guy even brought in a possum he had caught.

Pets all have one thing in common: they all pee and poop. And some scratch and bite. And you absolutely cannot rely on their human masters to assist them in these bodily functions. Before my no pets' manifesto,

I would find tenants who had gone off for a weekend leaving food and water for their dog, but no way to get rid of it when it passed.

Stinky!

And once a carpet is soiled, it's almost impossible to completely eradicate the smell.

And fleas! I was in the building once when Mary was going in to clean out a room. I heard an ungodly scream and found Mary frantically swatting at her legs which were black with the little critters. Whole house extermination.

When we arrived, Mary met us at the door. "I walked by Billy Bob's door and the smell damn near knocked me down," she snarled. "That boy's either dead or got a cat in there. I can smell a cat a mile away."

"Let's go take a look." I said. And the three of us climbed the stairs to #9.

Mary was right. Halfway down the hall our noses started to burn. I knocked on the door, "Open up, Billy Bob. It's me, Walt."

No answer.

"OK then," I said. "Willie's here and if you don't open this door, I'm going to have Willie do it for you."

"Oh all right," came the reply and we heard the deadbolt click. Billy Bob opened the door and we were nearly overcome with the stench that hit us in the face. I looked in and saw not one, but three cats curled up on his bed. The litter box in the corner was so full that no self-respecting cat would use it, so they didn't. Little land mines were scattered throughout the apartment and a bowl of sour milk sat curdling in the corner.

"Billy Bob," I said, "I think you know what this means. This is a violation of your lease. You and your buddies are going to have to move."

"But Mr. Williams," he pleaded, "I like cats."

"I like cats, too, you asshole," Mary chimed in, "How about we exchange recipes?"

"Ok, Mr. Williams." Billy Bob said. " I'll be out as soon as I find another place."

Nope! Been there, done that. They never seem to find another place.

"Well, Billy Bob," I said, "I don't think that's acceptable. We can either do this the easy way or the hard way. You can either pack up your stuff, and you and your friends are on your way, no harm, no foul, OR, I can call animal control and they will come out and take your cats to the pound. And when they see how you've been caring for them, they will certainly file a complaint for cruelty to animals. Your choice."

He thought for a minute and said, "Ok, I'm packing."

"Wise choice! I'll just leave Willie here to make sure you don't forget anything."

"Oh man, Mr. Walt." Willie wailed. "I stick around here much longer, I gonna have to shower fo a week jus to get de stink off me."

I never enjoy the role of the tough guy landlord, but I learned a long time ago, if you let the creeps run your building, the good tenants will all move out, and soon you have nothing left but a building full of creeps. That's how slums get started.

Mary and I went downstairs leaving Willie grumbling in the hall. "You hurry up and get yo' skinny white ass outta here befo' I puke."

I sat down in Mary's apartment and we talked about the Riddler case. She had been following it in the paper and Willie had given her his version of events. I shared with her the latest riddle, 'What's black and white and red all over, 9/6, B-2.'

"Well, hell," she said, "the first parts easy." I been doing puzzles and riddles for years. That one's as old as the hills. I'm surprised you didn't get it right away."

"OK, enlighten me," I said.

"It's a newspaper, silly." she replied. "The print is black on white paper and when people get it, it's read all over. See, read, not red. That's what fools you. But I don't know nothing about that last part."

"Ok," I said. "9/6 sounds like a date. B-2 might be the section and page number. Do you still have last weeks newspapers?"

"Yep, got them tied in a bundle waiting to put them out on recycling day." she replied. "Let me go get them."

She returned with the stack of papers and I shuffled through them until I found the September 6th edition. I turned to the second page of section B and looked at the column headlines. Then I found it.

"Rival syndicates vie for territory in Northeast Kansas City." The article went on to say that while Northeast had, for years, been under the control of the Italian mafia, Russian mobsters had been making inroads. Prostitution, bookmaking and protection rackets that had once been run by the Italians were now under the Russian influence.

It all fit. The import company's primary overseas contacts were in Asia and Eastern Europe. It wasn't a stretch to believe that Blanchard and Grissom had fallen under the influence of the Russian mob. They had strong-armed the partners into printing the money and laundering it through the export company.

I could imagine Blanchard and Grissom wanting out of the deal, and the mob hanging Blanchard was a warning to Grissom. They, of course, set it up to look like a suicide to divert attention from themselves.

Grissom, fearing for his own life, burned the printing warehouse to bring the operation to a halt, and went into hiding. But where are the engraving plates? Two Kansas City guys would certainly not have the resources to produce quality plates, so the mob must have supplied them.

Ah yes! Grissom has the plates and he's holding them hostage to protect himself and his family. His message to the mob would be, "You hurt me or my family and you'll never see your plates again."

So now, they are at a stalemate. Grissom is in hiding with the plates and the mob is trying to find both.

Probably, at the time they fired at Ox and me, they didn't know Grissom had the plates and they didn't want us locating them in the burnt rubble.

The pieces all fit. But what now?

I saw Willie escorting Billy Bob and his menagerie out the door to a waiting cab.

Good Riddance!

I thanked Mary, and Willie and I headed home. We had to roll the windows down to blow the stink off of Willie. He wasn't a happy man.

The next morning, I showed the Captain the newspaper and told him my theory on the case. He agreed and said he would pass the information on to the task force.

Just as Ox and I were leaving, an officer brought in another letter. The note inside read:

"Now you have the pieces of the puzzle. I'm sure you can put them all together. You must know they are looking for the engraving plates. They will be put where no one would think to look. Everyone wants this to be over. The next riddle will tell you where the plates will be. Use this information to catch the Russians: 'The man who invented it, doesn't want it. The man who bought it, doesn't need it. The man who needs it, doesn't know it.' Good Luck! But hurry! Time is running out."

We, of course, had no idea what the riddle meant. Each time, we had to let the words rattle around a bit and then brainstorm to try to make sense out of it. Then, it struck me. Who solved these riddles? Ox and Willie and Mary and the Professor, that's who. I pointed this out to the Captain and told him I had an idea. I wanted to get all these good folks together and see if we could come up with an answer. He agreed.

I told Ox to pick up Vince and come to my apartment. I called Maggie and told her I would pick her up. I called Mary and told her that I would pick her up. I called the Professor and told him to come up to my apartment. Now that I had my team in place, we would put our heads together and figure this thing out. I did a quick mental calculation. Together, we had over four hundred years of experience.

The Russians don't stand a chance.

CHAPTER 27

WE ALL GATHERED TOGETHER in my apartment. I ordered pizza and as we sat there snarfing pizza and slurping soda, I looked around at our little group.

In addition to Ox and Vince, our honest to goodness cops, there was Willie, a sixty-six year old street hustler who had helped capture the Gillham Park Mugger and solve a riddle. There was seventy-five year old Mary, tough as nails but with a heart of gold. She helped take down Louie at the Seniors' Prom and had solved a riddle. There was the eighty-five year old Professor who, with his wit and wisdom, had kept us heading in the right direction. And, of course, Maggie, my sixty-six year old sweetie, who's always by my side, lifting my spirit, licking my wounds, and telling me how great I am.

Although they will never wear the blue and carry a badge, these are the real heroes. This is my team. They will never be an official part of the City Retiree Action Patrol, but in my mind they're Honorary C.R.A.P.ers.

Roy Rogers had Gabby Hayes. The Lone Ranger had Tonto. Marshall Dillon had Chester. Batman had Robin. Walter Williams has the Crappers, and they're scrappers, every one.

"All right," I said. "It's time to get down to business. We have a riddle to solve. We know this riddle will give us a clue as to the location of the hidden engraving plates. Let's take the first line. 'The man who invented it doesn't want it.' So it has to be a physical object of some kind. But why would someone invent something they didn't want to use?"

"Well, that's easy," Mary said. "There's all kinds of stuff out there that people have invented and hope they never use. Somebody invented the thing they use for a colonoscopy, but who really wants a camera stuck up their butt?"

Good point.

"Then what we're saying is that the thing is useful or needed, but it has a negative connotation for the ultimate user," I said. "Let's go on to the next line. 'The man who bought it, doesn't need it.' So whoever bought it, has purchased it for someone else's use."

"Yea," Willie chimed in. "It's like when your old lady sends you to de store for some of dem 'my time of de month' things. I buys em,' but I sho' don' need em'."

"I see your point," I said. "But that doesn't fit with the last clue, 'He who needs it, doesn't know it.' If your lady friend sends you to the store, it's because she knows she needs it. It almost seems to imply that the ultimate user needs whatever the product is, and someone else gets it for him, but he's unaware of it because he's unconscious."

"Or dead," muttered the Professor.

We all sat in silence as we let these words sink in.

I was running the clues over in my mind. "What would a dead man need that someone would buy for him, that the inventor hopes he never has to use? Dead people don't need anything. They're dead!"

"They need a place to rest," Ox said.

"A coffin!" we all shouted at once.

It fits.

The guy who invented it sure doesn't want to use it. Someone has to buy it for the dead guy. And the dead guy sure isn't aware he needs it.

At least that's the theory.

Who do we know that's dead? Blanchard!

The note said that the plates would be hidden where no one would think to look and that time was running out. Who would look in a casket? And Blanchard's funeral is two days away.

But how can we use this information to catch the Russians?

The next morning, Ox, Vince and I sat down with the Captain and shared our theory. We were at a loss as to how to use the information to lure out the Russians. We concluded that what we needed now was to have Clark Grissom come forward with the plates.

An officer came in with another letter addressed to me. We opened it, and it read: "I hope you were able to solve the last riddle. If you were, then you know you will need help and cooperation to catch the Russians.

Solve this last riddle and you will know who I am. If you are willing to grant immunity, you may contact me. If not, I will deny everything. 'You do not want to have me, but when you have me, you don't want to lose me.' Good luck!"

Here we go again.

The four of us sat and pondered the riddle. It's something you don't want to have, but if you get it, you don't want to lose it.

"I think the key word here is 'lose'," I said. "Not 'get rid of' or 'throw away' but 'lose.' Normally, if you lose something, you're not aware of it until you miss it, but the riddle says, 'you don't want to', and that implies knowledge."

"There's another definition of 'lose', Vince said. "Lose can also mean 'not to win' as in a football game."

"True," I said. "But that doesn't fit with the first part about not wanting it in the first place. Usually you want to play a game. What else can you lose, but really don't want in the first place?"

"How about a lawsuit?" Shorty asked. "You never want one of those, but if you have one you certainly don't want to lose it!"

BINGO!

Ox, Vince and I headed to the computer room and logged on to casenet.com. This is a website maintained by the Circuit Court that tracks past and pending lawsuits. At any given time, there are hundreds of civil suits pending so we each took a computer and started wading through the current cases, looking for something that would tie into the Riddler Case.

After an hour, with no success, I found it. The case read: Laura Grissom vs. Clark Grissom, Petition For Dissolution of Marriage."

Laura Grissom is the Riddler.

We reconvened with the Captain. It would appear that Laura Grissom had actually been in contact with her husband while he was hiding from the Russians. She had been safe because the Russians didn't want to take a chance on losing the plates.

The Grissom's wanted to come forward, but could not do so without implicating themselves in the crime, so Laura anonymously sent clues so that we could uncover for ourselves the seriousness of the situation. They were hoping the police would be willing to grant them immunity to bring down the Russian mob. If not, Laura could deny everything.

The Captain took the information to the Joint Task Force. They agreed to immunity in exchange for the plates and cooperation in bringing down the mob. The City Attorney drafted an immunity agreement and we were ready to set our plan into motion.

We had to contact Laura Grissom, but suspected that the mob would be watching the house for Clark and maybe even have the phones tapped. So we enlisted Maggie's help.

Maggie came into the station, and after we brought her up to speed, she made the call.

"Hello, Mrs. Grissom," she said in her most professional realtor voice. "My name is Maggie McBride. I'm an agent with City Wide Realty. We have a mutual friend, Walter Williams. Walter told me you were dissolving your marriage, and I know that can often involve liquidating your home. I would like to offer my services."

There was a long pause on the other end. In one sentence, Maggie had told her that Walter had solved the last clue and was ready to help.

"I might be able to use your services," she said. "However, being a business woman myself, I always like to have everything in writing. Do you have something in writing that would explain your services in detail?"

She was looking for the offer of immunity.

"Absolutely," Maggie replied. "I have a document prepared that I believe will meet all your needs. Perhaps we could get together at my office to discuss it, and if you don't mind, your old friend Walter would like to drop by and see you."

She agreed, and an appointment was set up for that afternoon.

We were gathered in Maggie's office when Laura arrived. When she entered, I shook her hand and said, "The Riddler, I presume." She smiled and nodded.

I asked her why she had sent all the riddles to me personally.

"You don't remember me, do you?" She asked. I shook my head. "Well, do you remember Laura and Jim Maxwell? You sold us our house twenty-two years ago. Jim passed away and I married Clark. I saw you and your C.R.A.P program in the paper and I remembered what a good job you did for us. I trusted you back then. I figured I could trust you now. It turns out, I was right."

Lady Justice has a long memory.

Who knew a sale twenty-two years ago would help bring down a crime syndicate twenty-two years later. It boggles your mind.

Laura Grissom had discovered her husband and Blanchard's involvement with the Russians. She wanted no part of it and told them so.

But they were in so deep they figured the Russians would never let them out alive, and of course, they were correct.

Laura wanted to distance herself from the mess, so she filed for divorce. The threat of losing his wife caused Clark to convince Blanchard to pull away. That got him killed.

So now, with the immunity, if we could wrap up the syndicate, the Grissoms could get back together.

This was our plan. We knew the Russians would be watching every move that Laura made, in case Clark contacted her. We had to expose Clark and the plates so that the Russians would make a move to nab them without endangering Clark. The Russians knew Clark was going to hide the plates, so we put together an elaborate scheme to draw them out.

Myron Blanchard's funeral was scheduled for the next day. He was a respected businessman, so the funeral would be well attended. Laura, of course, would be there so we knew the mob would be watching closely. Since Blanchard was murdered, police presence would be expected, so any Russian attendees in the crowd would keep a low profile.

We would arrange for Clark Grissom to make an appearance with a package under his arm. As he paid his last respects to his former partner, he would slip the package in the coffin, but do it so that it could be seen. We were sure the mob was aware that there was a BOLO out on Grissom, so we would take him into custody after he planted the plates, thus ensuring his safety.

The mob would know the location of the plates, but couldn't retrieve them with all the witnesses. The coffin would be buried and our hope was that the mob would unearth it in the dead of night to get their precious plates.

Our plan was to hide officers at strategic locations through out the cemetery and arrest the Russians after they unearthed the coffin and retrieved the engraving plates.

The task force decided to have both uniformed officers and officers dressed in civilian clothing scattered among the mourners at the funeral home. I was assigned to be in civvies.

Willie and Mary asked if they could come to the funeral. They had been such an integral part of the operation to this point, I didn't have the heart to say no. And with all the law enforcement on the premises, I figured they would be in no danger.

I pulled up in front of my building and honked. Willie came out decked out in a black suit and red tie. I don't think I've ever seen Willie in anything but jeans and a t-shirt. With his silver grey hair and fancy duds, I thought maybe I'd picked up Sidney Pointier by mistake.

He climbed in the front seat and I said, "My, you're really looking dapper, today."

"Well, you got to have proper respect fo' de dead," he said. "And besides, my johnson's all healed up from dat damn coffee and I was goin' to see Emma after."

Nothing like planning ahead.

We picked up Mary next. She came out in her best flowered muu muu and had a little pillbox hat on her head.

High fashion.

She climbed in the back seat and we were off to the funeral home.

As expected, there was a large crowd. The case had drawn a lot of publicity and those with morbid curiosity probably outnumbered the mourners.

We found a seat and the service began. Everything went as expected. The Minister comforted the family and in his sermon, he spoke of the promise of eternal life and how Jesus had given His life so that we might live. Then a beautiful recording of "In My Father's House Are Many Mansions" came over the loud speakers.

Willie leaned over and whispered in my ear "Mr. Walt, what do you think happens to us when we die?"

"I really don't have a clue," I said. "But I'd like to think there's something more for us to look forward to."

"Mr. Walt, " he whispered. "You know I done some really bad stuff in my life." I nodded, and he continued. "Do you s'pose de Big Guy is gonna hold dat against me?"

"Willie," I replied, "do you believe in heaven and hell?"

"Well sho," he said, "I'se afraid not to."

"You can't just take part of it," I said. "It's a whole package. And if you believe in heaven and hell, then you have to believe in the Big Guy who set it all up to begin with. And they tell us He's a loving and forgiving God who has mercy on those who have done bad things but have stopped doing them and turned their life around."

Willie sat quietly for a moment then he said, "Thank you, Mr. Walt." He saw me looking at him and he tried to brush away the tear that rolled down his wrinkled cheek without me seeing it.

I've never met a man with a bigger heart than Willie Duncan and if there is truly any justice in the afterlife, Willie will be OK.

The service ended and one by one the mourners filed by the open casket to pay their last respects. As the last person stepped away from the casket, Clark Grissom appeared out of nowhere. A gasp went up from the assembled crowd.

Clark approached the casket with a rose in one hand and a small package in the other. He laid the rose on the casket and slid the package in beside the body and stepped away.

The funeral director immediately stepped up and closed the lid to the casket as he had been instructed by the police.

When the Russians dug up the casket they were going to be real disappointed. They didn't know Grissom had been working with the cops. The real plates were in custody and the package contained a brick.

Officers came forward to take Grissom into custody and escorted him away.

The funeral director then announced that the service would reconvene at graveside, and called for the pallbearers to come forward. They picked up the closed casket and carried it to the waiting hearse.

As is customary, the funeral procession was led by motorcycle officers whose job was to clear traffic. Then came the hearse with the coffin, followed by the family car and finally the long line of cars carrying the mourners.

The funeral procession wound slowly through town and all was going as planned. As we approached a major intersection, the motorcycles sped ahead to block traffic from the crossing lanes. But a block before reaching the intersection, a large cement truck pulled from a side street and stopped in front of the hearse, effectively blocking it from the officers ahead.

Two men jumped from the cement truck, pulled the driver of the hearse out of the vehicle, climbed in, made a u-turn, and sped away in the opposite direction of the procession.

DAMN! The Russians had been one step ahead of us. Instead of waiting to unearth the buried coffin, they had hijacked it right out from under our noses. Why can't ANYONE follow a script?

Willie, Mary and I were a few cars behind the hearse. I pulled out of the procession, did a u-turn, and took off after the Russians. It's not too difficult to follow a hearse. It doesn't exactly blend in with the other vehicles. And when other drivers see a hearse, they will typically pull to the side to let it pass.

We were keeping it in view until we approached an intersection where a large yellow school bus pulled out from a side street. I laid on my horn, which was a mistake as it caused the driver to slam on his brakes right in the middle of the intersection. By the time we had sorted everything out and the bus pulled away, the hearse was nowhere in sight.

"I got me an idea," Willie said and pulled out his cell phone. He put it on speaker and hit a speed dial number. A woman answered.

"Yo, Maxine, dis is Willie. You still working de corner of Independence and Prospect?"

"Sho nuff," she replied.

"A big ole black hearse is gonna be coming yo way. Y'all seen it?"

"Sho did," she replied. "Done passed by here jus a few minutes ago."

"Thanks, Maxine," Willie said. "Oh, is Irene still working Independence and Benton?"

"Sho is," Maxine replied.

Willie hung up and pressed the next speed dial and another woman answered.

"Yo, Irene," Willie here. "You see a big ole hearse come by your corner?"

"He jus' passed," Irene replied. "Dat big ole thing turned into dat ole abandoned Sears warehouse buildin'. I thought dat was kinda weird, you know, but weird stuff's happenin' on Independence Avenue all de time."

Willie thanked her and we headed for the warehouse.

When Willie dies, I want his cell phone. Just think how much I could get for a phone with a stable of hookers on speed dial.

We pulled into the dock area of the old warehouse. The hearse was not in sight. They had probably pulled it inside of the building.

We parked and went to the entrance door, and of course, it was locked. There was a small window by the door and I looked around for something to break the window. Mary said, "Hold on, Walt," and went back to the car. She returned with her Hillrich and Bradsby. "I don't go nowhere without my bat," she said. "Especially if I think there may be scumbags around."

Like the Boy Scouts, Mary's motto is 'Be Prepared.'

I broke the window, reached in and opened the door. In the far corner of the big warehouse, we saw the hearse. On the dock was the empty casket and Blanchard's body.

"Dey done took him outta de coffin," Willie whispered. "Dat jus ain't right."

I turned to Mary. "You crouch down right here behind the door," I said. "These are bad guys with big guns and I don't want you getting hurt. If you move a muscle from here, I'll have to fire you."

"OK, OK, I got the picture," she replied reluctantly.

Willie and I slowly crept to the dock and open casket. No one was in sight. Then we saw a door that led to an inner office. The Russians were probably there opening their brick. They were really going to be pissed.

We heard footsteps coming from within the building. I frantically looked around for a place for us to hide, but there was nowhere to go.

"Willie," I whispered. "Quick, get in the casket!"

"Hell no!" he replied, "I ain't getting in no casket."

"Would you rather get shot and be put in one for real?" I asked.

"You got a point," he murmured and climbed in.

I slid behind the door and waited for the Russian to emerge.

Just as he came through the door from the office, the outer door opened and the silhouette of a large man with a gun appeared. They must have spotted my car and the Russian circled around to check it out.

"Boris," he shouted. "The car is empty and the window is broken. They must be inside."

As soon as the words left his mouth, I saw Mary spring from behind the door and with a swing that Micky Mantle would have envied, she whacked the Russian in the back of the knees. He crumpled to the ground and the next sound was a sickening 'Thump' as Mary landed a blow on his head.

Boris moved to the edge of the dock next to the casket, lifted his AK-47 and aimed it at Mary. I couldn't let Mary die.

I stepped from behind the door. "Boris," I said, "it's all over. The police are on the way. Why don't you put down the gun?"

"It's a long way from over," Boris snarled. "You're going to pay for what you have done." He lifted the rifle and I thought my law enforcement career was about to end.

Just then, Willie rose up from the casket right beside the Russian.

"Don' you dare hurt my friend, you Russie scumbag!" he shouted.

Now I don't care how tough you may be, the sight of someone rising up from inside a casket is bound to unnerve you. It distracted the horrified Russian just long enough for me to make a midsection tackle just as I remembered from my one day at football practice.

The Russian stumbled backward, tripped on the casket and went flying off the dock, landing with a 'Whuff' on the concrete floor below.

By this time Mary had joined us, and as she stood above the Russian with her bat cocked behind her head, I heard her say, "Go ahead, Sucker, make my day!"

Sirens wailed in the distance and soon the warehouse was crawling with police.

The Russians were taken into custody and their testimony along with that of Clark and Mary Grissom led to the arrest of the leaders of the Russian syndicate.

That evening, our group gathered together again to celebrate our victory. If an outsider looked around the room, all they would see was a group of old, grey, wrinkled people that society had cast aside and put out to pasture.

What I saw was a group of people that age couldn't conquer. People that were vibrant and alive. People who still had a contribution to make.

I thought of all we had accomplished, but I also thought of all that lay ahead. The world is full of evil and wrongs that need to be made right.

Lady Justice needs all the help she can get.

And I would be willing to bet that from all the resources that are available to her, Lady Justice would take a C.R.A.P. any day!

If you enjoyed <u>LADY JUSTICE TAKES A C.R.A.P.</u>, watch for Bob's next release in the summer of 2010, as Walt Williams and his band of Scrappy Senior C.R.A.P.ers bring down the 'Elvis Strangler' and find themselves knee deep in other hilarious misadventures as they give Lady Justice a helping hand.

For information on the expected release date, ordering details, contact information, Walt's favorite recipes and more about the author, go to Bob's website:

www.booksbybob.com

"I HATE SPIDERS!"

ROBERT THORNHILL, M.A.

At age 66, Bob has written his first book, <u>LADY JUSTICE TAKES A C.R.A.P.</u> from his own perspective and experience as a Senior Citizen.

While Walter Williams is a fictional character, many of his adventures and friends are anecdotal and based on Bob's real life. Bob holds a Master's Degree in Psychology from the University of Missouri-Kansas City, but his wit and insight come from his varied occupations: stock boy, postman, truck driver, social worker, landlord, and finally to thirty years as a realtor, most of which as Broker/Manager of one of the largest real estate companies in Metropolitan Kansas City.

He lives with his wife, Peg, in a log home on seventy acres about two hours from Kansas City, MO.

Website and contact information:

www.booksbybob.com

LaVergne, TN USA
30 September 2009
159387LV00003B/2/P